THE *Wallflower's* MIDNIGHT *Waltz*

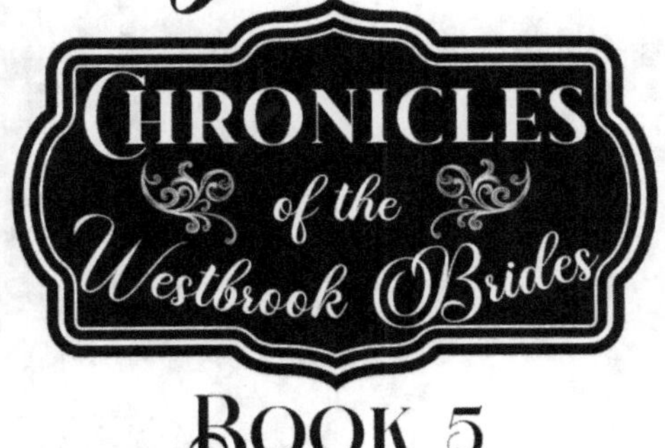

BOOK 5

Blue Rose Romance® LLC

"You intrigue
me, Angel..."

"Do you truly plan
on leaving
without
telling me
who you are?"

USA Today Bestselling Author
Sweet to Spicy Timeless Romance
COLLETTE
collettecameron.com
CAMERON®
Blue Rose Romance® LLC

PRAISE FOR...
THE WALLFLOWER'S MIDNIGHT WALTZ©

See What Readers Are Saying About
The Wallflower's Midnight Waltz!

★★★★★ "The author once again weaves her magic & adds her own brand of humour (which I adore) I devoured this delicious novella in a sitting."

— JANET

★★★★★ "This was a page-turner with a lot of feels. I loved the characters and I loved the story. I especially loved the epilogue. Woot!"

— KRISTI HUDECEK-ASHWILL

★ ★ ★ ★ ★ "What do you get when you combine a special story and Collette Cameron? A wonderful heartwarming romance that cannot be denied!"

— LORI DYKES

★ ★ ★ ★ ★ ". . . another sweet and romantic historical Regency with splashes of humor throughout! A definite 5 Stars Read!"

— PEGGY

★ ★ ★ ★ ★ "I love Ms. Cameron's marvelous ability to place the reader in the room with the characters. She crafted a superb description of the ballroom – from the "distinct aromas of body odor" to "the ping of rancid pomade," the "musty costumes, and cloying perfume" – oh, my nose was twitching just reading about it."

— TERRIE

THE WALLFLOWER'S MIDNIGHT WALTZ

A ROMANTIC OPPOSITES ATTRACT MYSTERY &
SUSPENSE FAMILY SAGA REGENCY ROMANCE

CHRONICLES OF THE WESTBROOK BRIDES
BOOK FIVE

COLLETTE CAMERON®

GET YOUR FREE BOOK!

THE REGENCY ROSE®

JOIN MY EXCLUSIVE MAILING LIST AND GET A FREE EBOOK!

Plus Sneak Peeks, Giveaways, Contests,
Exclusive Content and More...
P.S. I promise only good stuff ~ no spammy stuff!

Scan the following QR Code to join
The Regency Rose VIP Group Mailing List
and get your FREE BOOK!

Thank you,
Collette Cameron®

THE REGENCY ROSE®
VIP CLUB

*"The beauty of a woman is not in the clothes
    she wears, the figure that she carries, or
    the way she combs her hair.
The beauty of a woman is seen in her eyes
    because
that is the doorway to her heart, the place
    where love resides.
True beauty in a woman is reflected in her
    soul.
It's the caring that she lovingly gives, the
    passion that she shows and the beauty of
    a woman only grows with passing
    years."*

— AUDREY HEPBURN

ONE

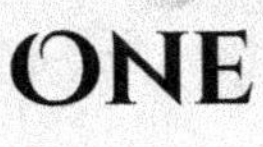

Hefferwickshire House
Cumberland, England
Late-morning

8 DECEMBER, 1826

Muscles taut and mouth firmed against the grimace struggling to contort his face, Peter Hartigan drew his mount to a halt in the grand mansion's courtyard. His heart slammed behind his breastbone like a hammer on a blacksmith's anvil, and despite the icy drizzle doing its utmost to penetrate his caped greatcoat, sticky sweat trickled down his spine.

He nearly reined Legend around and bolted for home.

Only sheer determination kept Peter from yielding to his survival instincts.

Teeth clenched, he tightened his thigh muscles around the horse.

As if sensing his owner's inner turmoil, the gelding side-stepped and huffed out an agitated breath.

Peter patted the horse's neck.

A crow cawed, its raucous call mocking Peter from the tree where it perched, watching him with beady, black eyes.

A dark omen?

Peter prayed it wasn't.

Bile, bitter and acrid, seared his throat as tension twisted in his stomach. Breaking his fast with nothing but black coffee hadn't helped, but so help him God, he couldn't have gagged down a bite of food this morning.

He had to do this.

I should have done it months ago.

Nevertheless, it did not make the quest any easier, for he knew full well he did not deserve a jot of mercy or compassion. Still, the guilt and self-castigation for something he did not remember plagued him incessantly, and even if he was unceremoniously tossed out of Hefferwickshire House on his arse, he meant to ask for forgiveness.

A year ago, when he'd first returned to Landford Park to convalesce, he'd been too ill to call on the Duke and

Duchess of Latham. Then, cowardice—pure and simple —had kept Peter away.

And shame.

Monumental, incapacitating, permeating shame.

For what could he say or do to make amends?

Nothing, except extend an invitation to the New Year's Eve masquerade ball he had decided to host as a ruse to call upon the Westbrooks. And pray that their graces, Althelia Westbrook, and her brothers would not see his gesture as the pathetic and wholly inadequate peace offering that it was.

At least the invitation, tardy and insufficient, was a start.

Grayish smoke spiraled upward from the house's many chimneys, adding a pleasant burning wood aroma to the otherwise dismal atmosphere.

Swallowing against the burning still clawing at his throat, Peter surveyed the house's familiar, elegant façade. Even in winter, Hefferwickshire House's gardeners kept the grounds and greens immaculate. The place fairly screamed blue-blooded aristocracy.

It had always been thus, and yet, unlike many members of *le beau monde*, the Westbrooks had always been warm, welcoming, and kind. Never superior or elitist in their attitudes or speech—something rare and admirable among the peerage.

How many times had he visited the Latham Duchy in his youth?

Too many to count.

At one time, the Hartigans and Westbrooks had been genial acquaintances and neighbors.

Until one night, drunken and heartbroken, Peter had made a horrendous, colossal, unforgivable, and yes—if he were wholly honest—cruel blunder. If only he could turn back time, could change that god-awful night that he'd publicly humiliated Althelia Westbrook.

Even in his foxed-to-the-gills state, he should have controlled his tongue. But wasn't that part of alcohol's seductive power? Intoxication rendered one's senses numb, one's will as pliable as warm Christmas taffy, and relegated one's manners and decorum to something only fit for the tosspot.

He skimmed another glance over the Duke of Latham's stately house.

Aware of the duke's righteous rage and fearing repercussions from the powerful peer, the Hartigans—merely landed gentry who hovered on Polite Society's fringes—had closed Landford Park within a week of the ghastly incident, with no intention of inhabiting the stately manor again.

To this day, Peter still wondered if the duke had *encouraged* his family's abrupt departure. Neither of his parents had ever said as much, and yet...

Bleakness, cold and merciless, speared him again, and he sighed.

Regret was a sneaky, unrepentant, and relentless thief.

No one had resided at Landford Park until Peter's return to convalesce last year.

Now with his parents deceased—Father from apoplexy and Mother, ten months later from a tumble down the stairs— Peter alone called Landford Park home.

Robert was in the navy, Harold seemed hell-bent on gambling and whoring his way across the continent, and their meddlesome and often malicious sister Leticia lived with a maternal aunt and, as always, left chaos in her wake.

Shutting his eyes for a moment, he squeezed the bridge of his nose.

He had no memory of the fateful evening that had catapulted his world into bedlam.

None.

Not even a whisper.

Had he ever?

His accident had stripped him of seventeen months of his life.

Cracking one's skull open on cobblestones after being tossed from a horse that had slipped on ice rather had a way of doing that.

Poof.

His memory...*gone*, like a cheroot's thin smoke trail in a gale's blasting wind.

The one good thing to come from his accident was that he'd given up imbibing in spirits—make that two blessings. He no longer pined for Meridith Peterson, the woman he'd proposed to, and when she had, to his absolute shock, refused his offer, he'd sought refuge in the bottle.

Peter remembered Meridith, but any emotion he might've felt toward her had long since dissipated. Had he truly loved her as he had believed, would she not still hold his heart, impaired memory or not?

Bowing his neck and pulling his mouth downward at the edges, he rubbed a finger across the rough scar running from his right cheek and across his temple before disappearing into his hairline—a constant, unapologetic reminder of his fallibility. Fat droplets plopped onto his lap from his hat's brim, and the distinct aroma of wet wool wafted upward.

His memory loss might not be permanent, the physicians said.

In truth, he'd regained a few snippets in recent months.

Nothing momentous, but enough scraps to encourage him.

Still, other recollections, taunting and teasing, drifted around the edges of his consciousness, shadows he couldn't fully see. His mind could no more grasp them than his fingers could vapor or fog.

Regardless, he had heard the painful details of the night he'd shamed himself and mortified Althelia Westbrook over and over and *over* from his sister Leticia, who still openly gloated about the anguish she had caused Althelia. Distancing himself from his malevolent sister was another reason Peter had returned to his childhood home.

Other well-meaning individuals, including Peter's London physicians, recounted past events in his life to help him regain his memory. A few malicious souls, such as his younger brother Harold, enjoyed reminding him of his idiocy merely to inflict guilt and make him suffer all the more.

Only last year Peter had learned that as a lad, Harold had shot Adolphus Westbrook's dog and left the poor thing to die. In a competition for callousness and cruelty, Peter would be hard-pressed to say who was the worst—Harold or Leticia.

And since Peter believed himself deserving of their contempt and judgment, he remained silent, refusing to defend himself. For there was no defense—never mind that he had been three sheets to the wind.

Debauchees always blamed others for their actions.

He refused to do so.

Trying to block out his self-loathing, he closed his eyes again for a blink.

Guilt was a blight upon his soul.

God, if he could only go back in time and change that fateful night.

How many hundreds—*no, thousands*—of times had he made that wish?

Bloody sot.

Perhaps it was a blessing that he could not recall his indignity of that wretched evening, for if others retelling the sordid tale caused him this much suffering, wouldn't his own memories be impossibly more unbearable?

His imbecilic behavior had destroyed a decades-old friendship, scarred a young woman—Althelia had left England for two years afterward—and sent him spiraling downward into a perpetual inebriated haze.

He became everything he had despised.

When he had recovered enough from his nearly fatal fall to travel, he yearned to return to his familial home. Ironic in so many ways, since his disgrace had begun there. Yet the silent rooms, sprawling greens, rambling hedgerows, and majestic oaks he'd played beneath as a lad soothed his tormented spirit as nowhere else could. Except, perhaps, the woodland thicket partially between Landford Park and Hefferwickshire House.

How he craved solace and peace.

As Peter dismounted, he glanced around, half expecting a dozen footmen or stable hands to come charging toward him, prepared to physically and mayhap even violently escort him from the property.

Instead, a maid, her head lowered against the blustery wind and skin-soaking drizzle, hurried toward him. Her dark blue woolen cloak flapped about her slender ankles as she held her hood in place.

She glanced up, her vivid blue eyes widening upon seeing him.

Rather than alarm, inquisitiveness flitted across her pert features, partially concealed by the hood draped over her hair.

Peter did not recognize her, but then he hadn't visited Hefferwickshire House in years. Servants came and went, though this one did not have a typical domestic's subservient mien.

"May I help you?" She glanced at his horse, and appreciation lit her eyes.

Not only did she recognize superior horseflesh, but she possessed an odd accent that he couldn't quite place.

"I have come to deliver an invitation," he said by way of an explanation.

Something usually delegated to a servant or sent by post.

"To a masked ball," he added.

"On New Year's Eve. The invitation is extended to all the Westbrooks."

Egads, man. Stop blathering.

Peter glanced toward the entrance, which remained firmly shut.

Had Simms recognized him and refused to open the door?

Did someone give the butler instructions of that nature?

"You do not look like a servant."

The maid's impertinent comment drew a reluctant chuckle from Peter.

The first in a very long while.

"I am not. I am Peter Hartigan." He pointed his attention and a finger toward Landford Park's chimneys, visible amidst the treetops on the horizon. "Hefferwickshire House's nearest neighbor."

An odd sound, a mixture of a gasp, a wheeze, and choking, made him jerk his head toward the servant once more.

She'd pulled the hood lower over her face, no doubt against the wind and damp. Only her chin, jutted at a rather mulish angle, remained visible.

"I shall take it inside." Distinct iciness leached into her voice as she extended her hand.

From her cool reception, Peter would be bound she knew who he was, even if he did not know her. That answered his question about whether the duke had advised his staff to rebuff him.

He had expected as much.

In point of fact, it was no more than he deserved.

He withdrew the thick invitation from his coat pocket.

The breeze buffeted his hat, compelling him to lift a black leather-gloved hand to keep it upon his head. "I had hoped to deliver it myself."

"The family is not home at present." The arctic wind held more warmth than the belligerent maid's frigid tone. "They attended Sunday services in the village this morning."

Rotten luck, that.

He should have expected their absence. The Westbrooks regularly attended services when in residence at Hefferwickshire House.

Peter hadn't braved the parish yet, though he had ventured to the village several times.

How could he enter a church where the cleric frequently preached about forgiveness, when he could not even forgive himself, let alone expect such amnesty from anyone else?

"Very well." He passed her the missive. "Would you also please convey my regards?"

She angled her head and gave the briefest nod. So brief in truth, her behavior bordered on insolent.

Her impudence ought to annoy him, but Peter couldn't begrudge her loyalty.

He'd have to wait and see if the duke and duchess

responded to his invitation. In truth, he held little hope that they would.

There was no point in lingering and becoming further soaked.

"Thank you." Peter swung back into the saddle, and with a finger to his hat, kicked Legend's sides.

As he trotted down the drive, a whisper carried to him on the wind.

"*Rotten lout.*"

However, when he glanced over his shoulder, the maid had already disappeared into the house.

Had he imagined her murmured insult?

TWO

Hefferwickshire House's foyer

SEVERAL NERVE-WRACKING SECONDS LATER

Sweeping the soggy hood off her head, Eva Westbrook entered the gleaming entry and inhaled the scent of freshly applied beeswax. Clutching the envelope in her white-knuckled hand, her heart pounding against her ribs like a Native American's celebratory drum, she glanced around, making certain she was alone.

She had nearly exposed her loathing when Peter Hartigan had revealed his name.

Only by biting the inside of her cheek—*hard*—had she checked her instinctive, and wholly unladylike, retort.

No one had mentioned how devilishly handsome the blighter was or that his warm, dark brown eyes resembled dual pools of melted chocolate. Even the puckered, pinkish-white scar marring the side of his face did not distract from his dashing good looks, and she loathed herself for even admitting she found him the least bit attractive.

She grudgingly acknowledged she now understood why Althelia had believed herself enamored of the clod. He was pleasant to the eyes—oh, very well, exceedingly pleasant—and no doubt had no shortage of feminine attention.

How had Peter Hartigan come by the disfigurement?

From the accident he'd suffered in London?

Murmurs and speculation about him swirled in the local village and even a few servants at Hefferwickshire House indulged in a clandestine whisper or two—though well out of Althelia's hearing.

Beatty, a fresh-faced chambermaid at Hefferwickshire House, particularly enjoyed gossiping about Peter Hartigan. Her sister held a similar position at Landford Park and fed snippets to Beatty, who couldn't wait to share the latest morsel with Eva.

Eva did not discourage Beatty's prattling.

One never knew what tidbit the loose-tongued maid imparted could be useful.

Was it good luck or ill fortune that she should be the

one to encounter the blackguard and that he mistook her for a servant?

Unmitigated bounder. Reprehensible rotter. Loathsome wretch.

The man who had wounded her beloved cousin had escaped repercussions for his cruelty. In truth, more than one of her Westbrook cousins had vowed to call the scapegrace out.

Uncle Garth, a man of estimable honor, had prohibited dueling of any kind. Neither he nor Aunt Margaret would allow their sons to be wounded, killed, or charged with murder, even to defend their only daughter's good name.

And so, Althelia had fled to America to lick her wounds.

Eva had spent many nights comforting her distraught cousin.

Had she been a man, Eva would have demanded satisfaction on the field of honor.

From Boston?

Yes, well, that would not have worked, would it?

Perturbed, she firmed her mouth. Her imaginary bravado had been for naught.

By the time Eva accompanied Althelia back to England, only to stay for an extended visit, the scandal and gossip had mostly abated, as Uncle Garth and Aunt Margaret had clearly known it would. In addition, word had spread that Peter Hartigan had suffered a devastating injury.

She supposed there were rules about calling out incapacitated oafs.

Pursing her lips, Eva stared at the elegant invitation.

Perhaps she could *still* avenge Althelia.

It did not matter that Althelia had blossomed into a confident and poised young woman while in America. Or that she no longer held any animosity toward Peter.

Though how Althelia could forgive the monstrous toad, Eva struggled to comprehend.

Regardless, she remembered the awkward and shattered young woman when she'd first arrived from England. Althelia had been so desolate and despondent those first months that Eva had despaired for her cousin's wellbeing and mental state.

Althelia's anguish had broken Eva's heart and evoked such empathy that she'd vowed more than once if the unlikely opportunity ever arose to seek vengeance on the man who'd caused such devastation, she would seize it.

Well, today the opportunity had quite fortuitously landed in her lap.

She'd developed a megrim and had ventured outside for a walk. When was the last time she'd experienced the ailment? Not for several years. Surely Fate had played a hand in the chance meeting.

People, especially men, getting away with vile and

abhorrent behavior without consequences, as if it were their due, disgusted her. Peter Hartigan must face consequences for his actions towards Althelia.

Somehow, *she* would see that he did.

"There you are, Miss Westbrook."

Eva slid the invitation inside her cloak before turning and summoning what she hoped was a pleasant expression —more on point, an innocent mien.

Simms, ever the dignified majordomo, approached with a measured pace. He searched her face, his fatherly gaze kind and concerned. "I hope you did not overdo it. Is your megrim better?"

"I am much recovered." Eva forced her lips upward.

She'd awoken with a vicious headache and had foregone attending Sunday services to stay abed. When her headache did not abate, she'd decided walking outdoors might remedy the persistent pain. It had mostly gone, although behind her right eye ached the merest bit still.

"The fresh air was just what I needed." She touched her temple. "I feel ever so much better."

At least, that was the truth.

She despised lying, but omitting information wasn't the same as fabricating truth, was it?

What harm was there if no one but her knew an invitation had arrived from that rattlesnake?

Even as she tried to justify her deviousness, her conscience railed at her.

You know better.

What you're plotting is not right, Eva Francine Angelica Westbrook.

No good can come from your scheming.

You have taken on another's offense.

If Althelia can forgive him, why can't you?

The answer to that question evaded Eva.

She did not know why.

Yes, she did.

She barely refrained from wrinkling her nose in contempt.

It was the unfairness of it all.

In this single case alone, she *could* make a difference.

"Excellent." Simms swerved a brief glance toward the closed door, and her heart skipped a beat.

Had he or another servant seen or heard Peter Hartigan arrive?

She prayed not.

Else, her plan would be thwarted before it had begun.

She assured herself that in a house this large, unless one was in a room with windows facing the front curving drive, it was unlikely that anyone had seen her encounter with Hartigan.

"Shall I have Mrs. Tastespotting prepare something for you to eat?" Simms asked kindly, redirecting his attention toward her. "Tea? Perhaps a slice of toast? A crumpet with preserves?"

Eva wasn't certain she'd be able to eat. Guilt had a way of souring one's stomach, for she'd already determined not to tell Aunt Margaret and Uncle Garth about the invitation.

Before Eva returned to America, she would exact revenge on Peter Hartigan. It was the least she could do on Althelia's behalf.

Eva would have to ponder exactly what that comprised, however.

But to do nothing...No, that was untenable. Injustice could not prevail.

Eva could not fail Althelia.

She would be her cousin's avenging angel.

Simms continued to gaze at her expectantly.

"Yes, tea and toast would be lovely. And in the kitchen is perfectly fine." Eva preferred the warm, cozy kitchen smelling of fresh bread, cinnamon, and herbs to the formal dining room. She fingered the clasps at her throat. "Just let me return my cloak to my chamber."

And hide the invitation.

"I can take your cloak, Miss Westbrook." Simms extended a hand ensconced in an immaculate white glove.

"That is very kind of you, but I have suddenly realized how famished I am and would appreciate you asking Mrs. Tastepotting to put the kettle on at once." Eva patted her windblown chignon. "Besides, I need to tidy my hair."

"Very good, miss." He dipped his noble chin and retreated toward the kitchen.

She allowed her shoulders to slump in relief before picking up her skirts and hurrying upstairs.

You are making a colossal mistake, Eva Francine Angelica Westbrook, her conscience chastised.

Her ethics bludgeoned her with the moral implications of her quest for revenge. And even as she acknowledged how destructive this path might prove, her desire to retaliate smoldered inside her, ready to burst into a blazing conflagration with the merest encouragement.

She could imagine her parents' horror.

Also, her aunt's and uncle's.

Likely dear Althelia's too.

A sudden wave of nausea engulfed Eva that she could not credit to her ebbing headache or empty stomach. Dread, apprehension, and self-recrimination assailed her simultaneously—a three-frontal assault. Pursuing this course of action was more than foolish—it was wicked.

Yes, but at least it was something Eva could do to confront the heartless and unrepentant cad and make him pay.

The truth was, this invitation to the masquerade ball was a godsend.

Well, perhaps not actual divine intervention—the Lord wasn't likely presenting opportunities for wallflowers to exact revenge on rakes—but it certainly wasn't something Eva could ignore.

As she flung her door open and whipped off her cloak, her mind raced.

A masked ball.

Perfect.

There were dozens of masks, wigs, and costumes stored at Hefferwickshire—almost an entire room full, in fact.

Peter Hartigan would not know it was her.

No one would.

She'd have to affect a British accent, but that should not be too difficult.

Then there was donning the costume and acquiring a means of traveling to Landford Park.

Beatty might be just the person to help with those tasks.

Wasn't the maid sweet on one of the stable hands?

And if Eva's identity somehow became exposed, so what if a few smudges marred her reputation? She wasn't the least worried about destroying her chances of marriage. This visit had never been about acquiring an English husband.

Some stuffy, puffed-up, pompous dandy she'd never quite be able to measure up to.

No, thank you very much.

Besides, she would leave for America in the spring.

A twinge of homesickness pricked her.

She missed her family. Other than Laine visiting England last summer, she hadn't seen them for over a year. Unfortunately, this extended visit hadn't helped her sort out or given her clarification about her future as she'd hoped it might.

Unlike many young women, at four and twenty, she enjoyed the status of a wallflower. Though she could dance and play the pianoforte—with minimal talent—she far preferred shooting guns, bows and arrows, or riding. Billiards was quite fun too.

And unlike the refined English roses, Eva was too outspoken, too brash, and too independent for British men. At home in Boston, there had been a few beaus— mostly her brothers' friends. No one had captured her heart, and it did not bother her in the least that she might end up an old maid.

Well, perhaps the tiniest bit, but Society allowed old maids to display eccentric, delightful, and precocious behavior that proper married ladies never could. That suited Eva just fine. The one thing she lamented was not having children. She believed she would have been an excellent mother, if perhaps a trifle unconventional.

She grinned at her reflection in the rectangular mahogany cheval floor mirror. Cheeks flushed, her dark brown hair slightly mussed from the blustery day, and her blue eyes alight with mischief, she appeared the epitome of a healthy country miss, except for the slightly naughty glint in her eye.

Indeed, she would make a most excellent spinster.

She needn't fret about experiencing lasting repercussions if her scheme went amiss. Boston was a long way from Cumberland.

But time grew short to exact her reprisal.

She narrowed her eyes at her reflection.

An avenging angel.

That was what she'd attend the masquerade ball as.

Now to determine just what she would do to Peter Hartigan.

THREE

31 DECEMBER, 1826 ~ QUARTER OF TWELVE

Resting an ebony-clad shoulder against the ballroom's door frame, Peter surveyed his hundred or so masked guests. Resplendent in their evening finery, draped in jewels, and swathed in the finest silks, satins, and wools available, they paraded about the ballroom.

While many attendees had come in costume, others such as himself and Leticia, had chosen to only wear a mask or domino. The mélange was a grand spectacle, indeed.

Hundreds of beeswax candles illuminated the sanded

dance floor and the ten-foot gilded mirrors on the ballroom's far side. He'd spared no expense for tonight—his re-entry into Polite Society—after nearly losing his life. Or so he explained to the guests as they greeted him earlier when they inquired about what had prompted his New Year's Eve masquerade ball.

Searching the ballroom again, he swallowed down another wave of disappointment.

The Westbrooks were not among the attendees.

Not the Duke and Duchess of Latham. Not Althelia Westbrook or her betrothed, nor any of the Westbrook brothers. He knew for a fact that several had been at Hefferwickshire House for Christmastide too.

A servant at the ducal manor was a sister to one of his maids, and he'd stooped so low as to encourage Milly to pry information from the other servant. He even rewarded her spying with an extra coin for her efforts.

That was how Peter had learned of Althelia's betrothal.

That she had found love brought him profound relief —not absolution, but knowing she was happy reduced his guilt a smidgeon.

Though Peter hosted the ball, an odd detachment, almost a sense of exclusion, cocooned him. As if he were an outsider and no longer a member of the elite society his parents had fought so hard to become a part of.

Sweeping his gaze over the crowd once more, he released a long, controlled breath.

Until this afternoon, he maintained a foolish hope that the Westbrooks would respond to his invitation. More than once, he'd considered riding over to Hefferwickshire House and inquiring in person if the Westbrooks planned to attend.

It wasn't done, of course.

Decorum demanded he await their reply.

That no one had even bothered to decline his invitation said a great deal.

Should he encounter them in public, they would no doubt give him the cut direct.

Was he stupid to try to rectify the wrong he had committed?

More on point, were his motives pure and not self-serving?

Was his desire for atonement genuine or merely absolution for his guilt? A guilt so weighty and cumbersome that he doubted Hercules could have stood under the monumental burden.

Yes, he admitted, clenching his jaw and curling his fists into tight balls. Selfishness motivated him in part. He *must* make amends so he could forgive himself and move on with his life as Althelia had done.

But it was more than that.

Rebuilding his reputation, regaining the trust of

friends and family, and earning redemption proved powerful catalysts as well.

He did not expect the relationship with the Westbrooks to be restored, but he had hoped for civility and a degree of healing.

For yourself or Althelia?

Why couldn't it be both?

Fear's talons clawed relentlessly at his stomach, and his palms grew moist in his white gloves.

I might not gain the redemption I crave.

Then what?

Would he turn back to the bottle?

Use spirits to dull his senses once more?

He gave a vicious shake of his head.

No. No. *NO.*

God forbid.

Absently running his finger over his scar, his attention alighted on a vaguely familiar woman attired completely in white, from the elaborate wig atop her head, threaded with strings of pearls and topped with several white ostrich feathers, to the slippers peeking from beneath the rows of lace along her gown's hem.

Many other guests had come in costume as well, though he couldn't discern exactly what her attire signified...until she turned slightly, revealing a pair of dainty, gossamer wings attached to her back.

An angel.

How appropriate.

Their gazes met across the room, and a nascent smile bloomed on her pink rosebud mouth.

A scintillating current jolted Peter to his toes. Long dormant masculine interest stirred deep in his belly. No woman had caught his attention since Meridith.

Who was this mystery woman?

Who had she come with?

Leticia sidled up to him, the usual smug half-smile curving her thin lips, doing nothing to enhance her plainness.

What had made his sister into such a vile human being?

He had not invited her to the ball, but somehow, she had learned of the event and had appeared two days ago with their arthritic, nearsighted, and with a propensity for flatulence that rivaled dairy cattle, Aunt Hattie Effingham in tow. He'd almost yielded to the burning temptation to send the troublesome baggage that was his sister, packing.

Still, this was Leticia's childhood home too, and he did not remember what part, if any, she had played in Althelia's humiliation.

"I am surprised but willing to admit your little soirée appears to be a success, brother." Leticia skimmed her critical focus over the milling crowd, an undercurrent of disdain shadowing her sharp features. "I cannot help but wonder if most of the guests came out of morbid curiosity. You have been such an enigma this past year."

Peter skewed an eyebrow upward.

Leticia always managed a backhanded insult beneath the veneer of a compliment.

A practiced pout turning her mouth downward, she slapped his arm with her maroon and silver lace fan. "I do not see the Duke and Duchess of Latham and their enormous brood. Do you suppose Althelia is still a blotchy-faced, frizzy-haired dumpling?"

Venom seeped into the last sentence.

Why did Leticia bear such ill will toward Althelia Westbrook?

He opened his mouth to tell her that from all accounts, Althelia had blossomed into a beauty—a fact Leticia would choke on as nature had not been as benevolent to her—but before he could speak, someone else did.

"No. She is not."

In unison, they turned to face the fascinating woman in all white.

Her pretty mouth curved upward pleasantly enough, but behind her white lace mask, blue sparks lit her eyes. Attention focused on Leticia, she deliberately opened and shut her fan, using the language of the accessory to convey her thoughts.

You are cruel.

Peter barely kept his grin of approval in check.

"Althelia has become a beautiful and confident young woman," the mystery woman said. "She is recently betrothed."

Leticia narrowed her eyes, her features gone hard. "I do not believe I have had the *pleasure...*"

So, she did not have a clue who the angel was, either.

The mystery woman slid him a sideways glance, a mixture of humor and challenge in the depths of her azure eyes.

"Ah, you would have me reveal my identity? *Tsk, Tsk.* Poor form." She flicked the fan back and forth as if chastising an errant child and shook her head, causing the feathers topping her wig to sway. "Surely you know better. It is not midnight yet. I shall keep my secret a while longer, I think."

"I do not believe we are unmasking until two," Peter offered, not the least disturbed by the eviscerating glower his sister speared him. Never mind that until five seconds ago, the unmasking *would* have occurred at midnight.

"So I can remain anonymous a while longer. Excellent." An enigmatic smile curved the angel's mouth upward. Nevertheless, the hardness in her brilliant blue eyes did not abate as she took Leticia's measure from head to toe.

Fascinating.

Leticia pursed her mouth tighter than a beggar's purse

strings before giving a toss of her head and stalking away without another word.

His sister always indulged her ill temper, not caring how unflattering it was or who she hurt with her cutting remarks. Their parents had constantly ignored her nastiness and pandered to her demands rather than address her unpleasant temperament. As a result, she'd become bolder and more malicious in her behavior over the years.

A bubble of laughter formed in his chest, and a chuckle escaped him.

It was about time his sister had her comeuppance.

It wasn't often that Leticia did not have the last word.

"Please disregard my sister's prying." Still grinning, he examined the pretty young woman. "She is unaccustomed to not getting her way."

The angelic figure lifted a delicate shoulder. "'Tis of no consequence."

The string quartet's lilting strings announced the midnight waltz.

"May I have this dance?" Peter extended his hand. "Unless your dance card is full."

That actual possibility sent his good humor plummeting to the floor.

A winsome smile bent her mouth again.

The faint essence of lilacs and jasmine wafted upward, teasing his nostrils.

Who was this delightful treasure?

"I have only just arrived," came her husky reply. "My dance card is empty."

And just like that, Peter's spirits soared once more, but not before he mentally filed away the mention of her late arrival. Hastings, his butler, would likely know who she arrived with, for surely a young woman this lovely had not come alone.

'Twould be scandalous to do so.

"Then I would be honored to be the first to partner you." For the first time in a long while, guilt did not beleaguer Peter.

Something far lovelier and tantalizing held his attention.

FOUR

SEVERAL ERRATIC HEARTBEATS LATER

*Y*ou are going to give yourself away. Calm down.

Eva silently ordered her frolicking heart to resume a normal rhythm while she concentrated on taking even breaths as Peter Hartigan led her onto the dance floor. For one awful moment, she'd feared the exposure of her ruse before she even put her plan in motion.

Not that she had much of a plan.

For days, she'd thought of little else, and the best she could come up with was to wait until the moment was right and then publicly humiliate him. Of course, such an opportunity might not occur at all.

Still, she must try.

Eva scarcely heard the string quartet or the guests laughing and murmuring as Peter bowed and she performed the perfunctory curtsy. Then he took her in his muscular arms and swirled her across the floor. And she, who'd always considered herself clumsy and awkward, glided swan-like over the sanded parquet, her slippers making little wisping noises with each graceful step.

Mayhap all these years, she had merely lacked the right partner, for dancing had never been this easy or enjoyable. It was as if she had wings on her feet.

"Have you a New Year's wish?" His voice held a raspy tone that hadn't been there before.

Yes. Yes, Eva did.

She wished this midnight waltz would never end, and for these few tantalizing and memorable minutes, temptation urged her to set aside her vow of vengeance.

"Not one I would share with a stranger." She canted her head. "Do you? Have a New Year's wish?"

"Until five minutes ago, I would have said no." A nascent smile tipped the corners of his mouth upward. "Now, I would know who you are."

That would not happen.

When she remained silent, he sighed and changed the subject. "You are acquainted with Althelia Westbrook?"

Peter smiled down at her, those chocolate-brown eyes behind his black domino smoldering in their intensity, and unexpected yearning curled in Eva's belly.

Good Lord.

He was devastatingly attractive, more attractive than any man she'd ever met. Despite being a self-declared wallflower, Eva was old enough and self-aware enough to recognize physical attraction.

She desired him.

The knowledge was as shocking as it was unsolicited.

How could she?

Such a traitorous response was untenable.

Self-castigation made her miss a step, but Peter Hartigan caught her and continued as if she hadn't stumbled.

His smile widened, exposing a flash of neat, square teeth.

Did he know what he did to her with that disarming smile, a sensual glance, a grazing touch of his fingertips?

Of course he did, and that was why she must be even more on her guard. Most especially with her untarnished virtue. It was one thing to have one's reputation smudged and tainted, but another entirely to become a *soiled dove.*

"I am." She would not give him any more than that. The less said about Althelia, the better.

"So secretive," he murmured, a speculative gleam entering his eyes. "I quite like a good puzzle."

That would not do.

Somehow, he'd turned the tables on her.

"Do not waste your efforts on me," Eva quipped, quite pleased with how calm and confident she sounded when a dervish whirled inside her.

Truth be told, she should not have jumped to Althelia's defense earlier, but when she heard that harpy, Leticia Hartigan, besmirching her beloved cousin, long-festering anger and animosity reared their gnarly, pointed heads.

"I am truly glad she is happy. She deserves it." Unexpected melancholy flashed across Peter's sculpted features, and his somber gaze slid beyond Eva, a muscle working his jaw.

His sincerity took her aback.

Why would someone who had been so cruel care about his victim's happiness?

Wouldn't he exult in Althelia's despair as his mean-spirited sister appeared to do?

Eva studied his firm, angular chin, the merest hint of dark stubble shadowing his chiseled jaw.

Why couldn't he be an ugly-as-the-devil troll who smelled of rancid cheese and dirty feet? Unwashed body and bad breath? Instead, he epitomized rugged, virile masculinity, and she was helpless to resist the magnetic draw between them.

"You intrigue me, Angel," he murmured in a tone she felt sure was designed to melt her bones.

Some avenging angel she turned out to be.

Peter met her scrutiny with an equally potent appraisal.

Something unnamed but compelling unfurled in her belly, spreading behind her breastbone and then to every pore in her body.

As they danced, she couldn't pull her regard from him. Their gazes had fused, and she could almost believe he was as entranced, as mesmerized, as she.

But isn't that what rapscallions and libertines did?

Like spiders, they enticed their victims into their webs until their unsuspecting prey became snared, helpless to escape.

Then why the apparent remorse of a few moments ago?

Nearby, a woman laughed, high-pitched and artificial. A man's seductive chuckle followed. For the life of her, Eva couldn't bring herself to divert her attention from Peter to see who they were.

Nothing but the two of them mattered in this moment.

"Have we met before?" Peter murmured, still holding her gaze captive. "We must have done. I feel certain I know you."

Only with the sheerest concentration did Eva keep from stumbling again.

How could he possibly recognize her?

He had only seen her once before, and she'd made certain to drag her cloak's hood low on her head.

Perhaps he voiced what she was also feeling?

The inexplicable attraction that defied explanation and logic.

"For shame. You are attempting to discover who I am again, Mr. Hartigan."

Tilting her head, Eva examined his features. They did not bear the jaded, worldly countenance one expected of a dissolute. But then, he had surprised her since they met.

What gentleman delivered an invitation to a ball in person, especially in December's inclement weather?

He smelled positively heavenly too. Most unfair and making it increasingly difficult to remember her purpose here tonight.

She breathed deeply, inhaling his essence.

Castilian soap, starch, sandalwood, and perhaps the merest hint of neroli.

Wonderful and sensual.

"I have partially lost my memory," Peter said matter-of-factly. He angled his dark head, the candles' glow casting him in a golden light. "The scar on my face is from an accident I had a year-and-a-half ago, causing a gap in my memory. Sadly, if we met during that time, I cannot recall." He half closed his eyes. "A circumstance I deeply regret."

A wave of unanticipated pity washed over Eva.

She'd heard about his amnesia, of course.

Beatty was quite the most obliging chinwag. She'd even assisted Eva in dressing tonight, agreed to cover for her if anyone inquired about the megrim that sent Eva to bed early, kept watch while Eva made her clandestine exit, and with the help of Beatty's beau, arranged transportation to and from Landford Park.

"No memory at all?" She searched his face, trying but unable to fathom the erasure of a year and a half of her life.

Did he remember what happened with Althelia?

Or...would he use his amnesia to pretend he did not?

"A few wisps, but I am almost a complete blank from the month before I left Landford Park until I came out of my coma after the accident. I was not expected to live, but I am hard-headed." A self-effacing, humorless smile arched his mouth. "Some say I ought to be grateful I cannot remember. I am chagrined to admit that I was not at my best during that time frame."

"But you remember Althelia?" Eva asked, fearing she'd give too much away. "The other Westbrooks as well?"

"Indeed. I have known the Westbrooks for decades.

We used to be on friendly terms." Sadness tempered his half-smile. "They attended the last ball hosted at Landford Park, although I have no recollection of that night or the months thereafter."

He does not remember.

FIVE

A COUPLE OF UNNERVING SECONDS LATER

Eva's mind raced.

This changed everything.

How could she exact revenge on a man who could not remember what he had done? The very act of vengeance should remind a person of their offense and punish them.

She should leave.

Now.

This had been a ridiculous quest from the onset.

But Peter's hand at the base of her spine marked her as surely as if he'd placed a fiery hot brand upon her flesh, and though they both wore gloves, the heat of his hand permeated the fine silk and traveled in undulating waves up Eva's arms and across her shoulders.

She hadn't prepared for this sensual onslaught—hadn't known she would need to.

It made no sense that she found a man attractive whom she was supposed to loathe. Although summoning her distaste at this precise moment proved most difficult. One thing was certain—Eva hadn't counted on her feminine reaction to him and would have to be on her guard all the more.

"Well then, I'll just have to wait until two o'clock to discover who you are," he purred into Eva's ear, his breath a warm caress that sent another shudder rippling through her.

Good Lord.

When she'd first arrived at the ball, she'd taken refuge near a pillar, both to observe Peter Hartigan and to summon the nerve to approach him. He seemed oblivious to the many women sending him flirtatious glances from behind their elaborate masks, or sashaying by and posing to display scantily clad bosoms.

That earned him a tiny morsel of begrudging respect.

According to Althelia, Peter hadn't been aware of her youthful infatuation, and his sister had been responsible for orchestrating the mortifying debacle. A fiasco that was also meant to humiliate him. Althelia's ability to forgive Peter still baffled Eva.

But then Althelia had found everlasting love, and Eva supposed love did indeed cover a multitude of sins.

Nevertheless, because of her propensity for nastiness, Eva couldn't like Leticia Hartigan.

At all.

The woman fairly radiated bitterness, superiority, and envy. Undesirable characteristics in any person, but even more unfortunate in one whom nature hadn't seen fit to bless with physical attractiveness. It left her with few redeeming qualities.

"I confess you have me at a disadvantage, Angel."

Peter twisted his mouth into a charming grin, and Eva nearly tripped again. The Almighty ought not to bless men with such dashing good looks who, when they smiled, nearly blinded women

His scar did nothing to detract from his striking looks. No, in truth, if anything, the imperfection gave him a dashing, swashbuckler mien.

Masculine temptation personified.

Eva was only flesh and blood, after all. How could she, a mere mortal, resist such enticement?

"The guests' identities are not strictly secret," he whispered, his tone slightly huskier and decidedly sexier than it had been moments before. "I promise not to tell anyone who you are."

"I..." Eva's mouth went dry as hearth ash, and she

licked her lower lip before clearing her throat. "Yes, well. I prefer to remain anonymous."

His face fell, and he appeared like a crestfallen child, denied a sweet or biscuit.

"Nay." Bursting into laughter, she shook her head and shook a finger at him. "You shall not sway me."

He grinned again, that alarming upward sweep of his firm mouth that caused her knees to unhinge and her pulse to race. "It was worth a try."

The waltz ended, but Peter did not release her hand. "Please join me for supper? Then another dance?"

Eva cast an uneasy glance around.

Had anyone noticed the marked attention he paid her?

Across the crowded ballroom, Leticia Hartigan scowled at Eva.

No surprise there. Althelia said Leticia bore grudges.

A frazzled maid hurried past Leticia, and she grabbed the girl's arm in a cruel grip. The servant winced and almost dropped the tray she carried. Her sharp features twisted in irritation, Leticia spoke to the maid, who turned a wary glance toward Eva.

She shook her head.

Leticia leaned closer to the servant and snarled something else. The maid gave a quick nod, and then, ducking her chin to her chest, rushed away the moment Leticia released her.

A little shiver scuttled up Eva's spine.

"You haven't answered me, Angel."

She dragged her attention back to the man at the center of her indecision.

Eva should refuse Peter's request.

She should go.

It was the sensible thing to do, especially since she no longer had a legitimate reason to stay. In truth, she should never have come. But even as her common sense encouraged her to do the practical thing, her heart yielded to desire.

She would stay and savor every second with Peter.

However, as soon as supper was over, she must leave.

"All right," she conceded. "But I must leave straight after dining. I cannot stay for another dance."

Peter tucked her hand into his elbow and guided her toward the ballroom door. "Why do I get the impression that you plan to escape before revealing your identity?"

Because that was exactly what Eva intended to do.

Must do.

She would put this night behind her as well as her unattainable pursuit of revenge.

It had been a fool's errand.

She comprehended that clearly now.

Except she couldn't regret her impulsiveness entirely. She'd seen a side of Peter Hartigan she'd not have believed he possessed had she not witnessed it herself.

He wasn't a bad sort.

Not a bad sort at all, and had they met under different circumstances, he might well have been the man to win her wallflower's heart.

SIX

Near the open veranda doors

JUST OVER AN HOUR LATER

Peter could scarcely recall what he ate. Yes, he'd heaped food upon the china plate, lifted the fork to his mouth numerous times, chewed, and swallowed. However, his entire focus remained trained on the ethereal creature beside him, which made concentrating on his meal impossible.

Too bad, too.

He'd spared no expense on tonight's meal. He'd even brought in a French chef to assist Landford Park's cook with creating the scrumptious delicacies Peter favored.

Still, he must have eaten his fill, for his stomach felt quite full.

Having also taken refreshments, the orchestra played the first few strains of a lively country dance. Amidst laughter and conversation, men and women took their places in parallel rows.

Peter wasn't of a mind to dance.

He'd far rather steal a few moments alone with the woman who'd captivated him from the instant he'd set eyes upon her.

"Shall we take a turn about the veranda?" He gave a pointed stare toward the shadowy terrace, illuminated by flickering torches where several other couples already wandered. Like him, they may have overindulged and needed to walk off a portion of their meal, or perhaps they sought a bit of reprieve from the ballroom's cloying fug and heat.

For all the guest's finery and attention to their elegant plumage, distinct aromas of body odor and sweat lingered in the stale air. Combined with the ping of rancid pomade, musty costumes, and cloying perfume, the stench was enough to make a person retch.

In any event, he would use any excuse to spend more time becoming acquainted with the enchanting creature who, from all appearances, had crashed his masked ball. A discreet inquiry to a footman, who conferred with

Hastings, Landford Park's butler, confirmed that the imposter had not arrived through the main entrance.

Peter couldn't summon a jot of irritation at her boldness. Her refreshing brashness had even caused him to temporarily forget the Westbrooks' snub this evening.

What an unexpected but most welcome gift.

With concentrated determination, he tucked all musings about his neighbors into a nook at the back of his mind. He would not ruin the moment by fretting or stewing about something he had no control over. Later, when his charming guest had gone, he would re-focus his attention on that problem.

Somehow, he must find out who this captivating, angelic enchantress was.

Hesitation shadowed her brilliant azure eyes as she cast an uncertain glance around before focusing her attention on the terrace. "I have stayed too long already."

Many balls lasted into the wee morning hours, so her anxiousness to depart, further raised his curiosity. Perhaps, she'd attended the ball on a whim or a dare and was afraid of being discovered and damaging her reputation. A bored Society miss, one slightly unconventional and seeking a bit of excitement, might agree to such an unconventional challenge.

For certain, this woman was an enigma.

A delightful, complex paradox.

Every now and again, her accent changed the merest

bit; the inflections triggering a niggling familiarity Peter could not place. He blamed that on his unreliable memory and still healing brain.

"I really should go," she demurred, but he detected contrition at her refusal.

"Five minutes. I swear, not a second longer." He placed his hand over his heart in a theatric gesture a Drury Lane actor would have envied. "Then I'll let you go, with the deepest of regrets."

"Are you always so dramatic?" Amusement swept her mouth upward as one dark eyebrow arched high. "Or are you attempting chivalry?"

"No, to being dramatic." Peter gave her a sideways smile. He had smiled more tonight than in the entire last year. "I concede you do bring out a flair for gallantry I did not know I possessed."

"Why do I find that hard to believe?" She laid her white-gloved hand on his extended forearm.

"Five minutes, Mr. Hartigan. Not a half-second more."

"Upon my honor." He managed a somber tone when inside he was turning joyous somersaults.

"*Hmm.*" There went her eyebrows again, elevated in skepticism.

Her hair must be dark, given the sable arcs framing her large blue eyes.

What Peter wouldn't give to see her entire face.

Once outside, she lifted her face heavenward and drew in a deep breath.

Peter's breath hitched at the vision she presented, silhouetted in the flicking shadows, as otherworldly as any heavenly being. Mayhap she *was* a heavenly visitor...sent to bring succor to his tormented soul.

Clouds blocked the stars, unsurprising this time of year, but at least it wasn't raining or snowing. A breeze had whipped up in the last few minutes, making it chilly outside.

She did not seem to mind, however.

"This is quite refreshing. This gown is terribly heavy and hot, and the wig? It is sweltering, and it itches." She laughed, a throaty, melodic laugh as she gestured to the wig she wore. "I am grateful I did not live a few decades ago, when tall wigs adorned with all manner of oddities were all the rage."

"I quite agree." Thank God that fashion had not reemerged.

Grinning and revealing the neat row of pearly teeth, she gave him a sideways glance. "I have seen a portrait of my grandmother with a wig which contained a birdcage, complete with a dove inside."

Peter had seen a similar portrait somewhere.

But where?

"Egads." He chuckled. "Was the poor thing alive?"

Cocking her head, his angel regarded him, much like a

bird herself, before lifting a delicate shoulder. "I do not know. I certainly hope not."

After steering her toward the terrace's far end, Peter turned his back to the few other intrepid guests still braving the frigid air and rested his hip on the ornate stone balustrade. He only had minutes to discover who she was so he could see her again.

He *must* see her again.

How long had it been since he'd laughed this much? Experienced unfettered joy, and yes, the peace he craved? Or felt such an instantaneous and potent connection with another person?

The former, not in a very long while—the latter?

Never.

No one had ever affected him so profoundly—not even Meridith.

"Do you truly plan on leaving without telling me who you are, Angel?"

The words left his mouth of their own accord, as if the cry of his heart must be spoken aloud.

Palms resting on the balustrade, she stared out over the rolling greens. Her throat worked, and she gave a reluctant nod. "I must. I am truly sorry."

Peter touched her hand, and when she did not resist, he took the dainty appendage into his.

She met his gaze then, and in the muted half-light, he detected wistfulness shimmering in her azure eyes.

Why the secrecy? he wondered for the umpteenth time.

Was she ashamed that she'd come without an invitation? Or perchance it was as he'd considered before...her reputation would be in shreds should it become known. Surely she could tell him if he vowed to keep her identity a secret.

He glanced over his shoulder.

Only two couples wandered the other side of the terrace.

A curtain covering the library's mullioned windows shifted slightly. Likely an amorous couple taking advantage of the window seat. Not an uncommon occurrence at gatherings such as these.

"Even though I know you feel this inexplicable connection too?" He turned her hand over and caressed her wrist with his thumb.

A rush of air escaped past her parted lips. "Y...yes."

"Why?" He lifted her hand to his mouth, and with their gazes locked, brushed his lips across her knuckles. "Why deny us whatever this gift is? Believe me when I tell you, I have never experienced anything remotely similar."

He placed her palm over his heart. "You have already captured my heart."

Once the words left his mouth, Peter could not deny their truth.

This angelic creature had, indeed, snared his heart.

Utterly and completely in a mere two hours.

Impossible. Inconceivable. Implausible.

He could summon dozens more words to describe the absurdity, yet it changed nothing. Had he not experienced this miracle, he would have scoffed at anyone who proclaimed they had.

"You should not say such things," she whispered, though pleasure lit her eyes.

He leaned nearer, so near, he could see the rapid pulse at the juncture of her throat and collarbone, and could once again smell her floral perfume.

Her eyelashes fluttered closed, creating dark fans atop her alabaster cheeks.

Sliding a finger beneath her chin, he tipped her face upward.

"Look at me, darling." Emotion rendered Peter's voice husky.

Her eyelashes trembled before she slowly opened her luminous eyes.

She appeared guileless and unpretentious.

"Do not call me that, Peter. I cannot be your darling."

Her lips were mere inches from his.

All Peter had to do was lean over a little more and he could taste their sweetness.

How he wanted to taste those plump, ripe lips.

Some might consider her mouth too large.

Not him.

Besides, her sunny smile could light up a moonless, midnight sky.

"What are you so frightened of?" he probed. "Can you explain?"

"I cannot. Please do not ask me to," she choked in a voice so tight and thin, he strained to hear her.

"Yes, I would like to hear your explanation too," Leticia's strident, mocking voice fractured the intimate moment.

A gasp tore from his angel's throat as she stiffened and yanked her hand from Peter's. Trembling like a leaf battered by a winter blizzard, she hovered as if ready to flee any second.

It did not take keen observation skills to deduce something petrified her.

Peter shifted and glared over his shoulder at his meddlesome sister.

"You are interrupting," he snapped.

Deliberately too, he'd bet his beloved horse, Legend.

Expression smug and arms folded over her less than impressive bosom, Leticia veered her malicious, triumphant focus between Peter and his tantalizing guest.

"This is the second time I have interrupted you on a terrace during a ball, just as you have been about to compromise a Westbrook chit." A satisfied feline grin contorted Leticia's face.

"*Oh, God.*" The mysterious stranger stumbled backward a few paces, one hand at her throat and the other over her mouth. Eyes wide as dual moons, she shook her head.

"Someone needs to save you from yourself, Peter, but I tire of the responsibility." Leticia gave an exaggerated sigh. "I suppose as the eldest, I cannot escape my duty, no matter how tiresome or burdensome."

The only thing she loved better than alluding that being the eldest Hartigan sibling somehow made her superior was her decades-old gripe and grousing that she wasn't the heir. That Peter had no control over their birth order mattered naught to his jealous sister.

She resented his birthright, and at every turn, made a point of voicing her displeasure.

Wait.

Did she say Westbrook?

Peter slowly stood, his mind refusing to comprehend what Leticia said. "Westbrook?"

His attention locked on the woman he'd nearly kissed less than a minute ago, who now stood trembling and ghostly pale.

"She is not Althelia." Of that, Peter was positive.

But she admitted she knew Althelia.

A chill that the wintery early morning air could not explain cooled his blood and a warning toll sounded between his ears.

"*Nooo*, you dolt." In a singsong voice, Leticia dragged

the words out, obviously enjoying the torment she inflicted. "*She* is Eva Westbrook. An American cousin. I have it on good authority. One of your maids is a sister to a maid at Hefferwickshire House. All it took was a little persuasion, and the story came spilling out."

She'd probably spent the last two hours haranguing and threatening every servant at Landford Park to gain that denigrating information.

Did she say American?

That explained the odd accent.

A few guests had gathered behind Leticia, making no attempt at discretion.

Bloody, bloody hell.

This was all Peter needed—another deuced scandal.

Fate seemed determined to rob him of his pride.

He faced the woman in white.

To her credit, she met his accusing gaze straight on.

"Are you?" he demanded, praying she said no, and proving Leticia was wrong, "Eva Westbrook?"

Her face awash with chagrin and anguish, Eva nodded.

A blend of emotions bludgeoned Peter.

Doubt. Confusion. Suspicion. Chagrin.

And finally, ire.

Shoulders hunched as much against the frigid air as the indignation thrumming through him, and to block out the titillated murmurs of his guests, Peter ground out one word. "Why?"

His raw, anguished tone reminded him of a wounded animal, and though his emotional transparency ought to have embarrassed him—that sentiment was trifling compared to the pain her duplicity inflicted.

"*I* know why." Once again, Leticia interjected, fairly bursting with gratification. "But you will not like it, brother dearest. When will you learn?"

A few more curious partygoers had detected something was afoot and meandered onto the terrace. By tomorrow, the news would have spread across all of Cumberland and within a week, London.

Fully aware she had the captivated attention of all present, Leticia gave a dramatic sigh, which nobody with ears or eyes could have believed was the least genuine.

"Shut up, Leticia." Done with his sister's machinations, Peter did not attempt politesse. "You have said enough already."

Tomorrow, he would banish her from Landford Park. If she wanted a single shilling from him in the future, she'd never return or trouble him with her presence again.

His entire life, he'd endured her vindictiveness, jealousy, manipulation, and malice.

Well, by God, he was well and done with her, sister or not.

The intrigued guests' whispers buzzed around the flagstone terrace, yanking him back to the moment.

He closed his eyes for a heartbeat.

How could this be happening...*again?*

Only this time, alcohol did not dull his senses.

Slowly, her attention riveted on Peter, her eyes incandescent with tears and remorse, the creature that had so mesmerized him—*no, bamboozled me like a wet-behind-the-ears, callow schoolboy*—backed away.

"Revenge, dear brother." Leticia's aggravating voice came from far away. "It was nothing but a madcap scheme about avenging Althelia, and you fell for it, hook, line, and sinker."

Her maniacal laughter raised goose flesh along his arms, and several men and women regarded Leticia with wary contempt.

All at once, Peter grasped the incontrovertible truth.

His sister was mad.

Utterly, stark-raving-queer-in-the-attic insane.

Nevertheless, he would deal with her later.

At present, it took every ounce of his self-control not to storm across the icy stones and shake the imposter.

How could he vow to love her and simultaneously feel such scorching rage?

"*Revenge?*" Peter choked on the word, pain eviscerating him. "Did your uncle, your cousins, or Althelia put you up to this subterfuge?"

"*No. No. No.*" She shook her head, the feathers waving wildly with her vehemence. "They had no part in any of this. They do not even know I am here. I never showed them the invitation."

Revenge.

It had all been a vicious ploy.

Devil take her.

What a consummate actress.

Had someone impaled Peter with a rusty, two-sided sword and mercilessly twisted the blade over and over, the agony could not have been more excruciating.

"I mistook you for a maid that day." Understanding finally dawned, and Peter lifted his head. "You are nothing but a Jezebel."

A ragged cry ripped from the avenging angel's throat and the next instant, the woman he'd fallen in love with at first sight spun around, raced down the steps, and tore across the greens, a ghostly apparition in the moonless gloom.

That was all she'd been.

A phantom. A specter. An illusion.

Not someone to fall in love with.

Or someone who could love him.

He was a fool. A deuced idiot. A bloody imbecile.

"Someone stop her!" Leticia shrieked. "She is getting away. Do not let her escape!"

At least Peter thought she shrieked.

Everything had become muffled and distorted. A thick

haze engulfed his brain, and piercing pain stabbed his scarred temple.

Of course, his sister would want to draw blood.

How like her. She did not recognize in herself what she accused others of.

"No." Peter raised a hand to his throbbing head as black spots danced before his eyes. "Let her go," he whispered weakly.

He never wanted to see Eva Westbrook again.

Likely, the she-devil had a conveyance nearby as part of her premeditated scheme.

His knees buckled as blackness engulfed him.

SEVEN

Hefferwickshire House's drawing room

THREE DAYS LATER ~ AFTERNOON TEA

One. Two. Three. Four...

Curling her toes until they might snap off in her kid leather slippers and fisting her hands in her lap until her nails would soon draw blood, Eva slowly finished counting to ten. Her facial muscles would crack soon under the strain of the forced smile she'd maintained for the past hour.

She took a sip of tepid tea, more for something to do than any desire for the beverage.

Her appetite had deserted her since fleeing Landford

Park three nights ago. A dull ache accompanied by nausea coiled in her belly, and nothing brought her reprieve.

Did guilt and remorse do that?

Why, oh why, had she taken it upon herself to play God?

Revenge was an ugly beast, as willing to devour the instigator as the intended victim.

This was a lesson Eva would gladly have forgone.

It did not matter that she'd already determined not to humiliate Peter. In those few wonderful hours, she had discovered a decent man. An honorable man. A fascinating, attractive man. One who made her wallflower's heart sing and, for the first time, consider what a future with someone might entail.

She would not place the blame entirely on Leticia Hartigan, either.

If Eva had not been at the ball, Peter would have been spared.

But I would never have known the real Peter, either.

The devilishly charming, and oh-so-tender man who'd vowed he'd given his heart to her.

And Eva had publicly obliterated the organ.

Decimated his pride—pulverized his trust.

For as long as she breathed, she would never forget the anguish etching Peter's face at her betrayal. Somehow, in that moment, she'd understood that he had been as much a victim as Althelia. His evil, calculating witch-of-a-sister had done that to him—not once, but twice.

Nay, likely many, many times over the years.

Thanks to Beatty's loose tongue, Eva's aunt and uncle had been awake and awaiting Eva's return from the ball at two in the morning. To redeem herself for betraying Eva, Beatty revealed that Leticia Hartigan had departed Landford Park the day before yesterday in an unmarked black coach and under the supervision of what appeared to be a nurse and physician.

Dear blabbermouth Beatty, also claimed Peter had collapsed on the terrace after Eva had fled. Since that night, he had refused all callers and retreated into isolation once more.

Eva had done that to him.

Unmitigated shame cudgeled her.

And here she had believed she was prepared to deal with the consequences if things went awry on New Year's Eve.

What a naïve ninnyhammer.

Fighting tears, she lowered her gaze and returned her teacup to its saucer with a calm and poise she was far from feeling.

After a moment, she regained her equanimity and perused the haughty guests, catching Theadora Brimley and her widowed sister, Lady Eugenia Montague, eyeing her from beneath their stubby lashes. She'd seen them at the ball. Both had eyed Peter like he was a French pastry they'd love to gobble up.

Summoning a brilliant smile, Eva gestured to the lemon bars. "Have you tried Mrs. Tastespotting's lemon bars, Miss Brimley? Lady Montague? They fairly melt in one's mouth."

The sisters swiftly averted their attention.

Point to me.

"Indeed. They are among my favorites." Althelia scooped up two, passing one to her betrothed, Owen Lockington.

"Thank you." He accepted the treat in his overly large hand and popped the entire sweet into his mouth. Chewing happily, he gave Eva an encouraging smile.

Bless Owen and Althelia.

Opposites in so many ways, Althelia and Owen had fallen in love in a matter of days over Christmastide.

Instead of being angry at Eva's brashness and impulsiveness, Althelia had hugged her. "I wish you hadn't taken it upon yourself to avenge me, Eva, but I know love motivated you."

Again, Eva skimmed her gaze over those assembled.

How much longer would they dawdle, hoping to hear a succulent tidbit they could spread about like marmalade on toast?

The Westbrooks had closed ranks around Eva and, though the intrusive guests tried many wily ways to bring the conversation around to the New Year's Eve debacle, Eva's family skillfully and oh-so-politely changed the subject.

More than one guest huffed a less-than-gracious sigh or swiftly schooled a vexed expression.

In the corner armchair, Grandmama had dozed off, her chin resting upon her chest. Her soft snores earned her tolerant smiles from her family, while the imposing guests exchanged uncertain glances.

No one dared criticize the dowager duchess for her slip in decorum.

Today, no less than nine members of the hoity-toity local upper crust had called at teatime. Three less than yesterday, but one more than the day before.

The duke and duchess welcomed each with a graciousness and warmth that escaped Eva.

Every last one had called at Hefferwickshire House on the pretense of wishing the duke and duchess a happy new year, but Eva and her aunt, uncle, grandmother, and cousins understood their true motives.

To see for themselves the outrageous American who had successfully taken Peter Hartigan down a peg.

Several of the visitors had attended the ball, but just as many had not.

What gave them the right to interrogate her?

To besmirch Peter?

Gossipy snoops. Busybodies.

Chinwags and tattlemongers, the lot.

Eva tried to beg off on the first day.

However, Aunt Margaret was not having any of it. "You created this muddle, Eva. You must deal with the consequences. Hiding away will only convey guilt and cause further damage."

Eva *was* guilty.

Unforgivably so.

Had she truly been so foolish as to believe she'd come through the debacle unscathed, should she be found out? She mightn't have suffered the mortification Peter had endured, but this constant remorse-induced torment was almost more than she could bear.

For the truth of it was, Eva wasn't cut from the same fabric as Leticia Hartigan. Cruelty wasn't part of her nature, and until she'd set her mind to avenging Althelia, Eva hadn't ever been deliberately malicious.

What was more, Eva recognized she'd grossly overstepped.

It was a wonder her aunt, uncle, and Althelia most especially, had forgiven her.

Eva had made certain to convey to all the Westbrooks her opinion that Leticia Hartigan had been behind the whole debacle regarding Althelia and that Peter, while inarguably in his cups, hadn't been aware of his sister's scheme that night any more than he had been New Year's Eve.

For the umpteenth time, Eva sneaked a sidelong glance at the ormolu mantel clock, still surrounded by Christmastide greenery and festive ribbons. Aunt Margaret insisted the house remain decorated until after Twelfth Night, after which the family was to take a trip to Owen's mining operations.

Only five minutes had crawled past.

Eva nearly groaned aloud.

Had time ever crept by so slowly?

A snail in molasses in January moved faster.

At last, the guests departed, their curiosity no more satisfied than when they'd arrived.

"I must attend to my correspondence," Uncle Garth said before kissing Aunt Margaret on the cheek and taking his leave.

Was one of those a letter to Peter?

Or had Uncle Garth already written him?

After learning on New Year's Eve that Eva had absconded with the invitation to the ball, her uncle mentioned it was past time he and Peter had a discussion and he'd vowed to pen a missive to his neighbor.

Eva stood and shook out her gown. "I think I shall go for a walk."

Anything to ease the anxiety thrumming through her veins. She'd always found the outdoors soothing, though normally, she chose to ride. Today, however, she wanted to walk until she was utterly exhausted.

Then perhaps she'd sleep tonight.

In the process of assisting Grandmama to her feet, Aunt Margaret glanced toward the window. "Are you sure, dear? It looks like it may rain."

"Let her go, Mama." Althelia wrapped a hand around Eva's waist. She gave a little squeeze and a reassuring smile. "We'll have a coze before supper when you get back."

Dearest Althelia.

Eva sent her a grateful smile.

"I, for one, am glad Eva served that bounder a dose of humiliation." Grandmama shook her cane, her ever-present assortment of bracelets tinkling with her movement. The dowager duchess did not take kindly to anyone hurting her family.

"Grandmama, he isn't the monster we thought him to be." Eva couldn't bear to hear Peter disparaged. "And I wronged him."

Terribly.

Even now, her unintentional contribution to his degradation clawed at her conscience.

"*Hmph.*" Grandmama harrumphed her disbelief. "If he was so eager to make amends, why did it take him this long to extend an invitation?"

"I told you." Eva couldn't believe she was defending the very man she'd suggested deserved castration not so long ago. "He was injured and has lost a portion of his memory. He doesn't remember what happened with Althelia."

Grandmama opened her mouth, but after a quelling glance from Aunt Margaret, clamped it shut.

"Go along dear, but do not stay out too long." Compassion shone in Aunt Margaret's eyes.

She and Uncle Garth hadn't lectured Eva on her imprudence, but their disappointment at her deceit left a lasting mark.

Tears filled Eva's eyes.

She'd made a horrible mess of everything.

Peter hadn't been wrong.

Something magical and unforeseen *had* sprung up between them.

Now she'd never know what might have been.

EIGHT

A Deer Trail in the Woods

LATER THAT SAME AFTERNOON

Am *I destined to be alone? To live my life in ignominy and plagued by contrition?*

Hatless and wearing only his favorite riding jacket as protection from the blustery day, Peter bent his neck, and with his hands behind his back, trudged along the well-used deer path through Ravenwood Grove. His boots crunching on an occasional twig, he contemplated his bleak future.

Lifting his head, he examined the familiar mossy, broadleaved woodland. He inhaled deeply. The pungent, earthy scent of decaying leaves and damp ground, combined with the musky, woodsy notes of the various trees, created a complex, aromatic atmosphere.

The peaceful copse, interspersed with late afternoon purplish-gray shadows, did not bring him the solace he sought today.

As a boy, he and his brothers had often played hide and seek amongst these stately trees. In fact, he, his brothers, and the Westbrook boys had spent innumerable hours in these woods pretending to be everything from dragon slayers to swashbuckling buccaneers.

Althelia had been too young to join them, and Leticia had not done so, declaring herself too elevated for such hoydenish behavior.

Peter had visited Hefferwickshire House often, and that's where he'd seen the portrait of the Dowager Duchess with the wig containing a birdcage. Amazing how he could remember that detail today when he couldn't do so a few nights ago.

Somewhere amongst the fairylike thicket lay an invisible boundary separating the two estates, but neither household had ever enforced the border.

Peter had always rather envied the Westbrooks' close-knit family. Even with twice the number of children as the Hartigans, and despite their elevated social status, laughter and love had always filled the Duke and Duchess of Latham's home.

Peter's parents barely spoke to each other, and when

they did, it was in the coolest, most reserved polite tones. From birth, they had relegated their offspring to nurses, governesses, and tutors.

His father assuredly never crawled around the drawing room pretending to be a pony, and his mother never twirled her children in a circle until both mother and child fell laughing and gasping onto the luxurious Aubusson carpet.

He'd never been jealous, per se, but had often secretly wished *he* was a Westbrook and not the Hartigan heir. A position his social-climbing parents made certain to remind him of with the regularity of the moon's rising.

Envious of his status as first-born-son, Leticia and Harold despised Peter, although both fully expected him to render them ongoing financial support. Only Robert, the youngest child and Peter's favorite, possessed any redeeming qualities, strength of character, and motivation.

The minute he'd finished his studies, Robert had bought a commission in the Navy and planned on making the military his career. Peter suspected Robert's choice had as much to do with exerting his independence as it did distancing himself from his relations, except for Peter, with whom he corresponded regularly.

Peter sneezed and then idly rubbed his scar before running his fingertips across a nearby fern's slightly leathery fronds. He puffed his cheeks out with a long sigh.

Lord, what a colossal debacle.

Leticia had descended into complete lunacy the night of the ball, and he'd wasted no time in arranging for her to live at a private asylum for the indeterminable future. The signs pointing to her deteriorating mental state had been there for years. Something about the events that night had sent her careening over the edge into blithering insanity.

Peter tightened his mouth against the grimace that tried to form when thinking of his sister. While he pitied her and would provide for her, he did not know if he could forgive her for her insidious meddling and premeditated cruelty.

Not yet, in any event.

Dear Aunt Hattie had departed for London with the haste of a woman several decades younger, declaring she'd had quite enough *bucolic respite*. A polite way of saying she wanted no further association with the hysteria and scandal at Landford Park.

Likely, she was relieved to be rid of Leticia's disgraceful and troubling presence as well.

Peter kicked a stone, relishing the minuscule satisfaction found in sending the pebble tumbling over the trail. It landed beneath a bracken fern's shiny, verdant fronds, and at once, a red squirrel's strident scold filled the brisk air. He glanced upward, glimpsing a fluffy tail disappearing around a stately oak's trunk.

In the distance, a doe raised her head, gazing at him

with soft brown eyes, before gracefully leaping over a fallen, moss-covered tree and bounding out of sight.

Peter drew in another lungful of refreshing air, relishing its fragrant, earthy scent. He far preferred the country to city life, where the noise and noxious smells never abated.

He released his breath in a whoosh.

His emasculating faint hadn't lasted long, according to Hastings who had the good sense to instruct the footmen to encourage the guests' prompt departure. When Peter had roused, he'd regained a chunk of lost memory, but still not the night that had altered the course of his life. According to the physician who attended him the next morning, nasty headaches often accompanied amnesia and recovered memories.

After the masked ball, he yearned to know the whole of what happened that long-ago night all the more. Now, with Leticia dicked in the knob, he likely never would.

Picking up a stick, he whacked it against the trees as he passed by them, much as he had wielded a pretend sword as a lad. Coming upon his favorite setting, a small glen with a few boulders strewn about, he sank onto a nearby rock.

As it had repeatedly and against his strictest commands not to, his mind turned to Eva Westbrook.

She had played him for an utter fool.

And yet...something deep inside him wanted desperately—*no, needed*—to believe that not all of that enchanted night had been artifice, that Eva had experienced the same enthrallment as him.

Thwack.

He struck the boulder he sat upon.

She *had* gazed at him with the same fascination.

And surely, no one could pretend such genuine remorse.

What difference did it make?

Thwack. Thwack.

He smacked the innocent rock, taking all of his frustration and anger out on the undeserving stone.

Repentant and tearful, Milly had confessed that Leticia somehow learned the maid had a sister employed at Hefferwickshire House. Leticia had planted a valuable piece of jewelry in Milly's chamber and then vowed to have the servant arrested if she did not tell her everything she knew about the Westbrooks.

Not only terrified of going to prison but also that her blind father and two younger brothers, who relied upon Milly's and Beatty's wages, would become destitute, she had reluctantly revealed Eva's identity.

Another employer might have sacked the servant for her disloyalty, but Peter knew his sister's viciousness. Without a jot of compunction, Leticia would have permitted the innocent servant's arrest. Besides, who was Peter to cast stones when sins tainted his soul?

In her eagerness to compensate for her betrayal, Milly revealed Eva was to depart England in March after having visited her aunt and uncle for over a year.

All this time, Eva had been at the adjacent estate.

So close, but she might as well have been on another continent or living in another century.

Had she not acted imprudently and stolen into the ball, Peter never would have met her.

Never would have given her his heart within mere moments of meeting her.

Like a rash, young buck.

In truth, until that momentous night, Peter would have been the first to scoff at such ridiculous twaddle as love at first sight.

Still, the point was moot.

Eva was not, nor would she ever be, part of his future.

Tapping the stick on his slightly muddy boot, he considered his alternatives.

He could remain at Landford Park, become a complete recluse, and perhaps even a bitter curmudgeon who chased everyone away while cursing and wielding a broom.

Or he could travel.

Alone.

Either choice held as much appeal as acquiring leprosy or the clap.

A soft rustling caused Peter to cast a casual glance behind him.

He froze, holding the stick in mid-air.

Joy and anger wrestled for dominance, and he couldn't draw a breath.

His heart galloped like an Ascot racehorse.

His stomach hurtled to his feet.

He blinked several times, no doubt looking owlish and stupid.

She stood there, wearing the telltale blue cloak he'd first seen her in.

NINE

The wind teased the tendrils framing Eva's face —yes, her hair was a rich dark whisky brown. It suited her better than the white wig. Uncertainty flitted across her features, but she stood her ground, meeting Peter's hostile gaze straight on.

How could he admire her fortitude while cursing her impudence?

She had to have seen him sitting here, so this meeting, like the one the other night, wasn't accidental either.

Was cheekiness an American trait?

After all, the colonials disdained the British aristocracy, believing all men were created equal. A notion Peter admired, truth be told. And yet, he'd wager Landford Park, that even in America, elitists existed who believed themselves superior and more deserving than most everyone else.

"Hello, Peter."

Did her voice tremble the merest bit?

Was Eva less confident than her poised composure suggested?

Good.

For *he* sure as Hades could not claim composure.

She rattled his senses as no other ever could.

Today, she did not use the forced British intonation of the other night, and her American accent's nasally inflection was undeniable.

Tossing the stick aside, he stood with an abruptness that bordered on aggression.

Her eyes widened, and she darted her tongue out to moisten the plump pillow of her lower lip.

Yes, she was far from self-assured, as she well should be after what she'd done.

"How did you know where to find me?" He pointed a severe glance down the path he'd just trod. "I doubt a servant told you."

No, indeed. He'd made it clear to his staff that he would tolerate no future incidents of disloyalty. Such betrayal would result in instant termination without a reference.

Puzzling her forehead, Eva tilted her head.

"I took a walk to clear my head, and I saw you in the distance." Swallowing, she averted her glance for a heartbeat, then swung it back to him.

Despite his inner turmoil, grudging admiration for her stalwartness rooted around his chest.

"I want to apologize, Peter."

A harsh, barking laugh burst from between his lips, sending a raven into a panicked flight.

The bird's alarmed cry echoed eerily in the woodland's ever-increasing gloom.

"Why?" Peter cocked a sardonic eyebrow, making no attempt to don the chivalry of the other night. "Did you not accomplish precisely what you set out to do?"

She drew in a deep breath, and he forbid his attention to linger on the gentle swell of her breasts as her lungs expanded.

The chill had reddened her cheeks and the tip of her nose. She clasped gloveless fingers before her, and he couldn't help but notice her white knuckles.

Did she shiver?

Or was she trembling?

No, she wasn't nearly as self-possessed as she affected.

A cad would have relished her discomfort.

He should savor it.

But, devil take it, Peter could not.

In truth, he'd give his life to keep her from suffering.

Even after her lies, manipulation, and the excruciating humiliation she'd brought upon him.

Didn't that make him the most colossal baconbrain to ever draw breath?

Dunderhead.

"I accept your apology, Miss Westbrook." Peter clasped his nape, rubbing the taut ropes that had taken up residence there. "You have alleviated your guilt. If there's nothing else, I shall excuse myself."

He swiveled to go before he gave into the insane urge to tromp across the damp ground, drag her into his arms, and kiss her until her full lips were as red as her fingertips and cheeks.

"That is not all, Peter."

When she said his name, he could almost believe she cared about him.

He raised his eyes heavenward.

Of course it wasn't all.

How much more do you think I can take, God?

He could not turn around.

Couldn't look into her lovely face and know that spark she had ignited into a blazing inferno in his heart and soul would gradually dim, until it sputtered out, leaving him the hollow shell he'd been before he met her.

No, worse.

Because he'd found love and lost it just as swiftly.

How heartless fate was.

Peter fisted his hands.

No, he would not touch her.

If he did, he would become utterly lost—his resolve, a feckless, malleable emotion.

"Have your say, if you must," he muttered in a voice so gravelly it sounded as if he'd gargled hot coals.

And of course, she must have her say.

She was Eva.

The bravest, most intrepid, most infuriatingly beautiful and irrationally desirable woman he'd ever met.

"When I arrived at the ball," she said, "I *did* intend to do something..." She paused at the admission. "But I did not know *what* I would do. I wanted to make you pay for hurting Althelia."

She had moved nearer.

Her heat beckoned to Peter across the space.

He flared his nostrils as the essence of lilies and jasmine wafted past his nose.

How long could he withstand this torment?

"But I realized almost at once that I had made a monumental mistake." Soft and earnest, her words came out in a rush. "You weren't at all the ogre I believed you to be. When I learned you did not even remember that night with Althelia, I decided to leave immediately."

So that was why she kept insisting she must go and why she wanted to keep her identity a secret.

"Only, you asked me to stay, and I wanted to, Peter. I

wanted to be with you, even though I knew I had no right." Her earnestness nearly undid him. "Because you also touched something in my heart that I did not believe I would ever feel...I had all but given up on feeling."

She laid her hand on his forearm, and Peter stifled a groan.

He was only human, after all.

And Eva Westbrook was everything his tormented soul longed for. She was succor to his wounded spirit, a balm to his scarred conscience, but most of all, she had given him hope of a future that wasn't filled with regrets and recriminations.

"I swear, I would give anything to turn the clock backward and to spare you the torment of that night, Peter."

She came around to stand in front of him, brave and brazen, and wholly intrusive.

Tenacity—another American quality.

It had served them well.

Regardless, Peter couldn't let her see his vulnerability.

His battered and bruised pride was all he had left. It proved poor company indeed, and an even worse bedfellow.

"But I cannot regret the time we shared, nor that I discovered what a wonderful man you truly are." Her voice caught and wobbled. When she spoke again, her tone was far from steady. "I hope someday you can forgive me, even though I know I do not deserve your forgiveness."

Clenching his jaw until he feared his teeth might crack, Peter refused to utter the words tapping at the back of his teeth.

I forgive you. I forgive you. I forgive you.

I still want to be with you, to make you mine for all time. It does not matter how we met or that I have only spent a few hours with you. It only matters that we are together. Please tell me you feel the same way.

She searched his face, her blue eyes sad and forlorn, sorrow and regret turning down the corners of her kissable mouth.

And then a fragile smile tipped her lips upward a fraction when he remained stonily silent.

"I understand, Peter. It is a lot to ask, and I am not positive that if our positions were reversed, I could absolve you, either."

She darted a swift glance skyward, her eyes narrowing as she peered through the canopy overhead. The soothing spattering of droplets pelting the leaves announced the rainfall's arrival that the laden pewter clouds had portended all afternoon.

After a moment, she brought her attention back to him. "I leave for America in a fortnight."

A fortnight?

But Milly said Eva sailed in March.

As if reading his thoughts, Eva lifted a delicate shoulder. "I thought it best to sail for home upon the next ship bound for Boston. I have brought enough disgrace upon my aunt and uncle, not to mention the scandal I have caused you."

No. Do not go. Stay.

I love you.

Even so, Peter could not form the words.

Could not utter the few syllables that very well could change both their lives and perhaps even give them a future that neither dared dream of. Because if he did—if he yielded to the ridiculousness of telling her he had fallen in love with her, and Eva rejected him and still sailed away —he'd likely never see her again.

And nothing could ever lift his soul from the black abyss his spirit would plummet into.

Nothing. Ever.

She turned and took two steps before looking over her shoulder. Vulnerability shadowed her pretty features as she pulled her hood over her dark, glossy hair.

Raindrops plopped onto the sturdy blue wool.

"I do not expect you to believe me, Peter, but I cannot leave without telling you, for it is unlikely we'll ever meet again..." Her eyes, deep indigo with emotion, she caressed his face with her gaze, and he felt it as surely as if she'd grazed a fingertip over his skin. "I have fallen teapot spout over handle in love with you. My heart shall ever and always be yours."

TEN

✦

Still in Ravenwood Grove

A FEW HEARTBREAKING SECONDS LATER

I *shall not cry. I shall not.*

Even though her heart had shattered, and with every step, another fractured piece fell into the damp earth, Eva pressed her lips into a tight ribbon and concentrated on putting one foot in front of the other. By nature, she wasn't a weeper, but leaving Peter and knowing she'd never see him again was more than she could bear.

Her ill-advised quest for vengeance had robbed her of something she never thought she'd experience.

Love.

An ironic laugh tried to burble up her throat, but she clenched her teeth to tamp it down, for if she opened her mouth, she feared a cry of anguish would emerge, not laughter.

What had she expected?

That Peter would haul her into his arms and declare his undying affection?

Could she have forgiven something as devious and earth-shattering so quickly?

In mere days?

Fool. Fool. Fool!

A tear slipped from the corner of her eye, but with a fierceness her part Roma grandmama would have been proud of, Eva blinked the moisture away. There were consequences to one's actions, and she would accept the repercussions of her stupidity without complaint.

"*Eva?*"

Peter's hoarse rasp barely registered before he spun her about and enveloped her in his iron-like embrace. He spoke into her hair at her temple, a guttural rumble that made her spirit soar with hope, even as her soul wailed because she'd caused him pain.

"Don't leave me. Please, I beg you, my darling. Do not leave me and go back to America."

Eva's knees buckled, and she clutched at his coat to stay upright. The tears did flow then, with abandon, but she did not care.

Peter wanted her to stay.

"I shan't leave." She tightened her icy fingers on his woolen jacket lapels. "Not if you wish me to remain."

The rain filtered through the treetops, splattering icy crystalline droplets onto them, but Eva did not care. With the setting sun, the woodland had grown dim, but even though the world around them had become cold, wet, and dark, the cocoon of his love kept her warm.

Peter wanted her to stay, and Eva would until the ocean ceased to caress the shore, until every grain of sand was no more, and until rain ceased to fall in England.

He held her tenderly in his arms, his damaged cheek pressed into her hair.

"I know it is impossible, and others will scoff and ridicule us. But I *know* what I feel."

He leaned back, his probing gaze searching the very depths of her soul in the muted light. "I would have remained silent and let you go, but when you said your heart was mine..."

It is, my love.

Irrevocably.

A rough chuckle reverberated in his chest. "I am a bloody fool."

"If you are a fool, then so am I." She offered a tremulous smile and cupped his cheek. "But I would rather be a fool in love than deny what I feel and live my life without you."

He pressed a fervent kiss into her palm, and the winter rain and wind did not cause the shudder which rippled from her waist, up her spine and trailed across her shoulders.

"I love you, Eva." A wry grin twisted his shapely mouth. "I shan't pretend to understand how this happened between us, but as surely as I breathe, you are my soul mate. Our spirits instantly recognized each other. I would stake my life upon it."

"It does seem incredible...like something from a fairy-tale or a dream," she whispered, still afraid to believe Peter had asked her to stay. And not only that, but declared his love for her.

He was right.

Others would not understand.

Sudden shyness and a smidgeon of doubt engulfed her.

"How can you forgive me so easily?" She shook her head, causing the hood to slip back even further. "I wronged you so."

He cupped her face in his hands. "Because, my dearest love, as I watched you walk away, my heart bled, and I realized, I could choose to harbor my anger and hurt at the expense of being with you, or I could let them go, and allow us a future together."

He kissed her nose, and she giggled.

"It was no choice at all, darling," he murmured, his mouth inches from hers.

Eva snaked her arms around his waist and stood on her toes.

"Kiss me, Peter."

In an instant, his hot mouth was upon hers, searing in intensity and wondrous in tenderness. He explored her mouth, tangling their tongues in a dance as old as time, and while dusk settled on the grove, she gave herself over to the magic of the moment.

Time ceased as she angled her head to allow him deeper access, the headiness of passion intoxicating and addicting. Plowing her fingers into his hair, her other hand splayed upon his broad back, she held onto him as if her life depended upon it.

"*Ahem.*"

Eva froze, then peeked over Peter's shoulder.

Uncle Garth and her cousins Fletcher, Leonidas, and Adolphus stood there.

None appeared the least amused.

No, from their rather ferocious expressions, they very much looked as if they'd like to throttle Peter before he could offer an explanation.

She lowered her heels to the ground.

"How many of them are there?" Peter quipped with admirable bravado.

"Four." She appreciated his attempt at levity but was certain her cousins and uncle did not.

Peter faced the Westbrook quartet, then in a brazen move Eva had not expected, pulled her to his side. "Eva and I are in love."

As if that explained everything.

And, in truth, it did.

Joy overwhelmed her.

Peter loved her. And she, who convinced herself she'd be content as an eccentric spinster, loved him too.

Her cousins' eyebrows wrestled with their hairlines before they exchanged flabbergasted looks.

"But you have known each other less than a week." Her cousin Fletcher verbalized the obvious.

"Three days, to be precise," Adolphus, the future duke, pointed out with taciturn logic.

"This is utter insanity." Leonidas snorted and swept his hand between Eva and Peter. "It makes Althelia and Owen's courtship seem the epitome of sensibleness."

Althelia and Owen had also fallen in love swifter than the family was comfortable with. Uncle Garth and Aunt Margaret had insisted they wait to exchange vows.

His countenance unreadable, Uncle Garth studied Peter from beneath hooded eyes.

This was the first time the Westbrooks had seen or spoken to him since Althelia's public disgrace.

"This is neither the time nor the place for such a

discussion." Uncle Garth shifted his focus to Eva. "Your aunt became worried when you did not return for your promised coze with Althelia before supper."

Eva gasped. She had forgotten. "It completely slipped my mind. I am so sorry."

A mocking grin contorted Fletcher's face. "I cannot imagine why."

"Be nice, Cousin." She squeezed Peter's hand and then stepped away from the protective shelter of his arm. "I must go. Say you will come to Hefferwickshire House tomorrow."

She'd stepped over the mark, inviting the Westbrooks' nemesis into their home, but how else could this feud be resolved? For as much as she loved Peter, she would not turn her back on her family.

Althelia must be warned, and Owen might very well take it upon himself to pound Peter into next December.

Peter veered his regard to Uncle Garth. "Is that acceptable to you, Your Grace?"

Please say yes.

"It is." Uncle Garth nodded, though his demeanor remained reserved and cool. "I shall meet with you at half of two."

It wasn't a request.

Neither was it an invitation to the midday meal or tea.

Still, Eva would not push the issue, and mayhap, if the meeting went well, her aunt or uncle would extend an invitation for Peter to stay for tea. Hopefully, none of the local busybodies would drop in unannounced, or Simms would have orders to turn them away.

At least Uncle Garth wouldn't have to write Peter a letter now.

Eva understood full well that she'd done what some might deem unforgivable—

fraternizing with the enemy.

Regardless, she did not need anyone's permission to marry Peter. She was of age.

Of course, she'd prefer her family's blessings.

Peter dipped his chin in deference.

"Until the morrow." After a half-bow and a lingering look that made Eva's cheeks burn, he turned around and, boots crunching, strolled away.

"Whatever can you be thinking, Eva?" Leonidas demanded before Peter had traversed more than a few feet.

"As I said, this is not the time to discuss today's events." Uncle Garth pulled her hood up. "Come, let's be away before we catch a chill."

It was only as she slid her hand into the crook of her uncle's elbow that Eva realized Peter had not asked her to marry him.

ELEVEN

Hefferwickshire Drawing Room

*FIFTEEN MINUTES PAST TWO THE NEXT
AFTERNOON*

Wearing one of her favorite gowns, a pretty, long-sleeved lavender frock, Eva pushed the lace curtain aside a couple of inches and peered toward the circular drive. She'd taken extra care with her appearance today. Pretty mother-of-pearl combs adorned her hair, swept into a new style, and Grandmama had loaned her a pearl necklace and earrings.

Peter hadn't arrived yet.

It did not help that the entire family had assembled in

the drawing room, sans Uncle Garth, of course. Eva had grown tired of explaining herself.

How could you explain the mystery of love to people who had never experienced it? Those who had, like her cousins Adolphus and Lucius, whose courtships had also been something less than ordinary, could hardly point a finger at her.

Except, the glaring elephant in the room was that Eva's heart had chosen a man loathed by the Westbrooks for over three years.

A winter storm had blown into the countryside this morning. A vigorous wind tormented the trees and shrubs while icy rain pelted the barren landscape.

Eva sent a furtive glance to the ormolu mantel clock before clamping her teeth upon her lower lip and resuming her sentry status.

What if Peter did not come?

What if he did not ask her to marry him?

Stop it.

Love is not fickle, and neither is Peter.

He will be here.

Cane in her gnarled, arthritic hand, Grandmama toddled over to stand beside Eva.

As ever, her abundant pendants and bracelets tinkled and clinked with her labored movements.

"I cannot think why you set your cap for that rascal," Grandmama said, her eyes owlish behind her spectacles.

"But never let it be said that I stood in the way of true love. You have my blessings, my dear."

A concession indeed.

Eva bent and kissed her grandmother's papery cheek. "Thank you, Grandmama."

Owen grunted something under his breath.

"*Shh*, my love," Althelia consoled. "If what Eva says is true, then Peter is as much a victim as I was."

A curricle approached, and tension eased from Eva's shoulders.

"He is here," she announced to no one in particular.

"I still may punch him in the nose," Lucius said, flexing his fingers.

"Lucius!" Eva glowered at him. "You will do no such thing. He has not had an easy time of it. Try to summon a jot of compassion."

His wife gave Eva a warm smile before turning to her husband.

"My brothers showed great restraint when they met you, and you abducted me, my love," she said in her lilting Spanish accent.

"That was different." Lucius clasped her hand and kissed her fingers. "I was protecting the Crown."

"I believe you nearly caused an international incident, did you not?" Leonidas mocked.

An ankle hooked over his knee, Fletcher scratched an

eyebrow and tipped his mouth into a smirk. "Exactly why I avoid romantic interludes."

Shaking his head, Adolphus chortled. "No, you don't. You just avoid commitment."

"Boys, that is enough." Aunt Margaret chastised them as if they were still lads in short pants. "Eva, dear, sit down. Your pacing is making me dizzy."

Eva's nerves had grown so taut she couldn't sit. Instead, she perched on the settee's arm near the fire and stared into the frolicking crimson and orange flames. "I know you think I am a fool, and that I do not know what I am doing. I cannot explain it, but I know that Peter and I are meant to be together."

The clock chimed three.

Eva turned to peer at the closed door.

It had only been thirty minutes since Simms admitted Peter into the house and no doubt led him directly to Uncle Garth's study. What she would not give to be a fly on the wall in the room.

The door handle rattled and her stomach leaped in anticipation.

She barely prevented a frown when Simms entered bearing a tea tray, followed by a maid and a footman, each carrying another tray.

"Do I smell fresh gingerbread?" Leonidas sat up, eager expectation on his face.

"Ah, tea." Aunt Margaret gestured toward the tea

table between the two settees. "Put two on the table please, and the third on the side table."

No sooner had Simms finished expertly arranging the tea service, than Uncle Garth strode in, accompanied by Peter.

Eva raked her gaze over him.

His expression gave nothing away.

"I see we are just in time for tea." Rubbing his hands together, Uncle Garth grinned. "Gingerbread? My favorite."

Had Simms put Mrs. Tastespotting up to that? Convinced the dear cook to prepare the family's favorite treats to put them in a more receptive mood?

She sent the kindly butler a grateful smile, and he winked.

The sly dog.

He had indeed conspired with Cook.

Uncle Garth waved a hand toward Adolphus. "Son, would you do the honors? Neither your wife nor Lucius's have been introduced to Mr. Hartigan."

Eva thought she might scream in frustration.

Adolphus dutifully performed the introductions, as perfunctorily as possible, before piling his plate high with dainties and settling back on the settee with a satisfied sigh.

Peter still stood, somewhat awkwardly, just to the side of an armchair. He cleared his throat before addressing

Althelia. "Please accept my most sincere and humble apologies, Miss Westbrook."

"Let's leave the past in the past, shall we?" Althelia tilted her head and gave a gracious smile. "Isn't that right, Owen?"

Owen's expression revealed he wasn't feeling nearly as charitable as his betrothed, but he managed a stiff nod.

None of Eva's boorish cousins offered to move to make room for Peter, so she stood, not caring what anyone thought, crossed to him, and took his hand. "You can sit by Grandmama."

"I would speak with you alone first." He gave nothing away with so much as a glance or a quirked eyebrow.

That stopped everyone mid-motion.

Uncle Garth, in the process of chewing a rather large bite of gingerbread, nodded his approval. He swallowed, then dabbed his mouth. "Yes. Eva can show you to the music room, although I would venture you remember the way."

"I do, Your Grace," Peter said.

Aunt Margaret set her teacup down. "Is everything as it should be?"

Now that was a loaded question.

According to whom?

Eva studiously avoided meeting her cousins' gazes, fully aware she'd see amusement, mockery, or cynicism in their eyes.

Giving his wife an indulgent smile, Uncle Garth speared another piece of gingerbread with his fork. "Perfectly fine, my dear."

Eva had never had the urge to shout at her uncle, but at this moment, his secretiveness had nearly pushed her to the point of rudeness.

"Come, Peter." Eva took his elbow.

Part of her desperately wanted to know what he had to say, and part of her was terrified of finding out.

Aunt Margaret raised a stern auburn eyebrow. "Leave the door open."

"Of course, Your Grace." Peter dipped his chin and guided Eva from the room.

Her cousins' lighthearted bantering carried into the hallway, making her miss her siblings. She'd always intended to return to America, but given a choice between that and staying with the man whom she'd given her heart to...Well, it wasn't a choice at all.

God had given her an undeserved gift, and Eva would be a fool not to seize it with both hands.

Though she and Peter had only to walk a few feet down the corridor, with every step, her trepidation increased. He remained silent the entire way, although he offered her a half-smile.

They'd barely crossed the threshold before she turned to him. "Something is wrong. I feel it in my core. Did Uncle Garth forbid you to see me? If so—"

"No, it is not that." Peter shook his head, his expression growing even more pained.

God, please don't let him have changed his mind. I couldn't bear it.

And yet, disappointment darkened his eyes and turned his mouth down. "But he says we must wait until your parents arrive from America to wed."

Eva gaped at him.

Peter *did* want to marry her.

"*That's* it? That's what has you acting so severe?" She nearly whooped but restrained herself before daring, "Besides, you haven't actually proposed."

He gathered her in his arms and pressed a kiss to her crown.

"Marry me, Eva. Make a future with me, please."

Her heart soared to the heavens with joy.

"Yes, Peter. Yes, I'll marry you."

Peter sighed into her hair. "I do not want to wait months to make you my wife, but I shan't elope with you. I must earn the duke's and your father's respect."

Wrapping her arms around his waist, she rested her head against his chest. His heart beat strong and steady beneath her ear. Eva sighed, more content than she'd ever been.

"I can wait, knowing we will be together. My feelings for you will not change, Peter. Not in a few months, not in several decades, not even after I leave this world. You are the love of my life—my soul mate. Forever and always."

He tilted her chin upward, and Eva was stunned to see tears glinting in his eyes.

This man who had been so wrongly judged was humble, honorable, and utterly marvelous.

"That is exactly how I feel, my darling." He caressed her cheek with the knuckle of his forefinger. "Our love may have come upon us suddenly, but it will endure for all time. I do not doubt that."

He lowered his mouth and captured hers in a searing kiss, sealing their troth and promising a love that surpassed human understanding. For their love wasn't just carnal yearning for completion, but it was the meeting of two souls, becoming one.

For now and all eternity.

EPILOGUE

Aboard the Whispering Zephyr
Boston, Massachusetts Harbor

EIGHT YEARS LATER

Holding his four-year-old son, Zachary, in one arm, Peter gazed out upon the hustle and bustle that was Boston Harbor. This was the first time since Eva visited her Westbrook relatives in 1825 for Christmastide that she'd been home.

They had been the happiest, most contented eight years of his life.

He had grown impossibly more in love with Eva with each passing day, effectively silencing the scoffers who predicted their whirlwind romance would not last. Not only had their union endured, but their marriage had flourished.

In the ensuing years, he had developed a genial relationship with Althelia and Owen Lockington and the Westbrook clan. Less satisfying was Leticia's continued confinement to an asylum with scant hope of her ever recovering her mental faculties, and Harold's death in a drunken brawl brought about when he'd cheated at cards. Robert visited as often as he was able, and last winter he'd taken a bride.

Still, those unfortunate situations did not detract from the blessings bestowed upon Peter.

"Papa, *this* is Mama's home?" Six-year-old Luke asked, wrinkling his nose at the pier's permeating stench. "It stinks."

"*Stinks*," Zachary parroted, then grinned and pinched his nose. "Poopy poop."

The child had the right of it.

A distinct odor of manure combined with fish and other strong, nostril-burning aromas created a most unpleasant miasma.

"No, dearest. This is only the harbor. Your grandparent's house is a few miles away." Shifting their sleeping eight-month-old daughter, Evelina, in her arms, Eva gave Luke an indulgent smile before shifting her attention to Zachary. "Zachary, darling, we do not say poop."

"Why?" Zachary was of an age where most of his conversations involved the word why.

Peter cocked an eyebrow.

Here we go.

"Because it is considered impolite and crude," Eva reasoned with practiced patience.

Zachary thrust out his lower lip. "Why?"

Peter jostled the child slightly.

"Because, young fellow, your mama said so, and she is a very wise woman." He winked at Eva. "She married me, didn't she?"

Luke rolled his eyes as he turned to grip the ship's rail and peer over the top. "See what you have done, Zacky? Now Papa will tell the story again of how he and Mama met and fell in love at a *maskrade* ball."

Eva sent Peter a private smile, love shining in her eyes. "You must admit, it's quite a romantic tale."

"It's *girly* stuff." Luke rolled his little shoulders. "Boys care about horses. And shooting and fishing and riding and archery—"

"All of which your mama does better than most men."

Including Peter.

While some men, particularly pompous sticks-up-their-arses-peers, looked down their long, haughty noses at Eva's less-than-feminine skills, Peter applauded them.

Her nonconformity is precisely what drew him to her in the first place.

Zachary laid his head against Peter's chest. "I like horsies too."

"There's Mama and Papa." Delight lit Eva's face and she stood on her tiptoes and waved like a six-year-old. "Oh look, Peter! Mynna, Laine, Emerson, Rogen, and Clarke came too."

She cut her sons a sidelong glance. "They are your aunt and uncles," she explained to the boys.

Peter hadn't met Eva's eldest brothers. Only Mynna and Rogen had accompanied their parents to England for the wedding.

Compunction prodded his conscience.

Eva had sacrificed much to remain in England.

As if reading his mind, she sidled closer.

"I know that expression, Peter Ronald Davis Hartigan."

Her smile would have lit a midnight sky, and for the ten-thousandth time, Peter wondered what he'd done to deserve her.

"No, I do not for one second regret staying in England to marry you." She leaned into his side. "Of course, I love my family and I miss them. But *you* are my heart. I cannot fathom my life without you."

Her eyes grew soft and misty.

She rarely cried, and that she permitted the display of emotion in public revealed just how true her words were.

Peter, on the other hand, had no problem with public displays, and without hesitation, lowered his mouth to hers for a very satisfying kiss.

"Look, Lukey. Mama and Papa are kissing." Zachary giggled and made a kissing noise. "*Kiss. Kiss.*"

"They always do after Papa tells the story of how they met." A tinge of disgust threaded Luke's boyish voice. "I suppose we had better get used to it."

Indeed, they had better because Peter did not intend to hide his adoration for his wife from anyone. He'd display it everywhere and at any time he dashed well pleased.

I hope you enjoyed
THE WALLFLOWER'S MIDNIGHT WALTZ,
following the romantic journey of
Peter and Eva.
If you'd like to leave a review please
scan the following QR Code.

SCAN HERE TO LEAVE A REVIEW FOR
"THE WALLFLOWER'S MIDNIGHT WALTZ"

Keep reading for a FREE PREVIEW of
MINUET AT MIDNIGHT
Book 6
Chronicles of the Westbrook Brides Series...

Minuet AT MIDNIGHT
CHRONICLES of the Westbrook Brides
USA Today Bestselling Author
COLLETTE CAMERON

West India Docks
London, England

MAY 1827 ~ LATE AFTERNOON

Pushing his cap back, the driver glanced around, his concern palpable. "The docks ain't no place for an unaccompanied lady."

"Yes, my aunt is meeting me." Primrose searched again for Aunt Rhodesia's familiar face. "We're sailing with the tide."

Two coaches, one bearing a gleaming crest and from which numerous crates and trunks had been unloaded and stacked on the dock, lay parked several feet farther down the crowded pier.

"Ye did say the *Sea Queen*?" The hackney driver removed his flat cap and after scratching his head and cramming the accessory back on his bald pate, he gestured toward the ship halfway between the hackney and the coaches.

"Yes." Of that, Primrose was certain.

She passed him a few coins, though she couldn't spare them. He'd been so kind and helpful, however. And after today, she wouldn't have to scrimp and save every penny anymore.

"Thank ye, kindly, miss."

Hands thrust in his trouser pockets, he took up a position a few feet away, making it apparent that he acted as her protector.

"I'll just wait with ye, miss."

At the speculative glances a few of the bolder men on the pier cast in her direction, Primrose couldn't ignore the slight tremor skittering up her spine. After working in Lyster's hostelry for over fifteen years, she ought to be as used to leering men as she was to ribald speech and bawdy jokes. Still, she gave the hack driver a grateful smile, welcoming his presence and appreciating his thoughtfulness.

A cat raced across the scarred wooden pier, a scruffy dog yapping in pursuit. Farther along the other end of the wharf, a bewhiskered gentleman assisted a stout lady up a gangway. A manservant and what must be a lady's maid trailed behind, bearing their luggage.

Rotating her neck to ease the tightness there, Primrose swept her attention up and down the pier.

Where was Aunt Rhodesia?

A plump man in a leaf-brown striped suit bustled around the front of the unmarked coach and, appearing disgruntled with his hands on his hips, surveyed the wharf. Upon spotting her standing uncertainly, a grin split his face, and he marched forward, his rotund belly leading the way like a plow before a horse.

"Primrose!" he hailed from several feet away. "It *is* you."

"Cousin Chesley?"

She peered behind him for Aunt Rhodesia and her lady's maid. Perhaps they waited in the coach or had already boarded the vessel. "Am I late?"

"Not a bit of it." Face flushed and his cheeks mottled red, he shifted his mossy-brown eyes here and there, unable—*or unwilling*—to meet her gaze straight on. He darted his tongue out and licked his upper lip.

Like a great toad.

Primrose couldn't regret her uncharitable comparison. Particularly as his unfortunate choice of a green waistcoat and absence of a noticeable neck reinforced the comparison.

"Shall we?" Still grinning, he extended his arm in the *Sea Queen's* general direction. Beads of perspiration dotted his upper lip and brow, and telltale dampness darkened his jacket beneath his arms, though it wasn't overly warm outside.

Aunt Rhodesia hadn't mentioned Chesley would travel with them, though Primrose supposed as her only son, it made sense. Nevertheless, a twinge of disappointment pricked her, and she had to remind herself that she was at Aunt Rhodesia's mercy and munificence.

Regardless, Primrose held no fondness for Chesley.

Spoiled rotten by his doting mother, he'd been unkind to her the few times they'd met as children, secretly pulling her hair and pinching her, though he was ten years her senior. He also lied constantly, often blaming her for his nasty antics.

From opposite ends, another pair of men rounded the waiting coaches—one tall and well-built and the other squat and broad. The first, with a dove gray hat atop midnight hair and his tailored ash-gray coat, reminded Primrose of a sleek greyhound.

In contrast, the second fellow, with his wide shoulders, thick neck, meaty face, and attired in a tan jacket and buff-colored pantaloons, more closely resembled a bulldog.

She concealed a grin.

The unfortunate but amusing childhood habit of occasionally comparing people to dogs entertained her.

As he had as a child, Chesley still resembled an obese pug with bad teeth and fetid breath.

Head tilted upward, the taller man spoke to the driver, unfastening luggage from the back of the coach bearing the crest, while the shorter, muscled fellow leaned against Aunt Rhodesia's coach with his arms folded.

Who was the latter chap, and why was he here?

He wasn't Aunt Rhodesia's coachman.

That ancient servant dozed in the driver's seat, his chin on his chest.

The hackney driver quirked a brow, silently asking if all was well.

"This is my cousin." She nodded to reassure him. "I shall be fine. I appreciate your consideration."

"My pleasure, miss." After putting two fingers to his forehead, the jarvey clambered aboard the hack and drove away.

Chesley had waddled ten feet farther down the pier. Since the last time she'd seen him, he'd put on a good stone—or four. A frown dragged his untamed eyebrows together over his beak-like nose.

"Are you coming, Primrose?"

Impatience and something slightly more sinister tinged his whiny voice.

The rotter didn't even offer to carry one of her bags.

So typical of cossetted and coddled Chesley—Aunt Rhodesia's one shortfall. Blinded by love for her son, she could never see his flaws, of which there were too many to count.

"Yes. Of course." With a little grunt, Primrose lifted her heavy bags and plodded forward.

Instead of directing her toward the gangplank, Chesley marched toward the coach.

A wave of unease tripped along her shoulders.

"Hasn't Aunt Rhodesia already boarded the ship?" she asked.

"*Pardon*?" Chesley half-turned, his face a mask of irritation. His expression cleared, and he shook his head. "No. No. There's been a slight change of plans."

He chuckled, a placating, artificial gurgle that raised her nape hairs.

"*Change of plans*? What sort of change of plans?"

Ten feet from Aunt Rhodesia's coach, Primrose slowed to a stop.

Again, unease warned her something wasn't as it should be.

The man in gray tossed her a cursory glance as he accepted a box from his driver. He possessed the bluest eyes she'd ever seen, fringed by thick, sooty lashes.

They rivaled the Highland summer sky or Loch Ness in June.

"Yes. Dear Mama mixed up the sailing date." Chesley held the coach door open. "The ship sails the day after tomorrow. She bids me fetch you home and apologizes that she did not come herself. Her arthritis is acting up."

Probably worse in her injured wrist.

Out of breath from trying to keep up, Primrose glanced toward her aunt's coach.

The bulldog man with muddy brown eyes had straightened and now examined her from head to toe with the intensity a cook might while selecting a prime piece of meat for supper.

Something definitely wasn't right.

Not right at all.

Though Chesley's story was plausible, warning bells clanged loudly in her ears.

Leaving her bags, she approached the tall stranger. "Excuse me, sir?"

What had she to lose with her daring?

Nothing, and much to gain if her intuition proved correct.

She would learn whether Chesley—a habitual liar— told the truth, and every womanly instinct she possessed shouted that he fibbed. Curiously, those same premonitions also assured her she could trust the striking man in gray.

Either her instincts were spot on, or she was in a bumblebroth up to her neck.

"*Prim—rose.*" Chesley fairly growled, dragging her

name out several syllables and pitching his voice high at the end. "Stop dawdling. *Get* into the coach."

The blue-eyed man turned, and she was quite certain he assessed her thoroughly in a heartbeat before skimming his cool gaze over Chesley and the bulldog.

"Yes, miss? May I be of assistance?"

He possessed a lovely voice, deep and rich like velvet.

No annoyance or irritation etched his face or threaded his tone, but rather an unexpected but wholly welcome sincerity.

"Primrose," Chesley snapped, all pretense at civility gone. "Mother *is* waiting. She shall become worried should we delay any longer. Don't bother this gentleman with your silliness."

"'Tis no bother to assist the lady." Flintiness entered the gentleman's eyes and voice.

His massive drivers descended from the coach and placed themselves on either side of him, expressing without words that they were there to defend him.

Who was he?

A gentleman, to be sure.

Likely a lord, given the coach's crest.

The bulldog had the unmitigated gall to approach her, his demeanor menacing and his oily, reptilian eyes sending an icy shudder up her spine.

"Better do as your cousin asks, Miss McKessick. You

wouldn't wish for your aunt to fret, now would you? It is going to rain soon too."

Stiffening, Primrose retreated two paces.

How dare he address her, let alone presume to tell her what to do?

They hadn't been introduced.

More unnerving, however, was why Chesley had revealed her name to a seedy stranger?

Furthermore, Scotswomen were well accustomed to rain.

Resisting the urge to hide behind the tall, blue-eyed figure just a few feet away regarding her with unexpected but appreciated patience, Primrose pointed toward the *Sea Queen* instead.

"I'm sorry to bother you, sir. But when does this ship sail, and where does she sail to?"

The handsome stranger puzzled his noble forehead before veering a sideways glance toward Chesley and the bulldog. He swept his keen gaze over her once more.

"The *Sea Queen* sails to Greece on the evening tide."

I hope you enjoyed this FREE PREVIEW of
MINUET AT MIDNIGHT
Book 6
Chronicles of the Westbrook Brides Series.
If you'd like to keep reading
please scan the following QR Code.

SCAN HERE TO GET "MINUET AT MIDNIGHT"

GIGGLES ARE GUARANTEED

COLLETTE'S CHERIS READER GROUP

If you love to chat about all things romance-book related and enjoy taking part in fun and engaging live events, contests, and giveaways join **Collette's Chèris VIP Reader Group,** my exclusive private book group on Facebook.

Giggles are guaranteed!

Hope to see you there,

Collette Cameron®

Please scan the following QR Code to join:

YOU ARE CORDIALLY INVITED TO JOIN
COLLETTE'S THERIS
VIP
READER
GROUP

DUKES COME CALLING

A Sensual Marriage of Convenience
Regency Historical Romance

FOR THE LOVE OF AN EARL (Wicked Earls' Club)

A Humorous Aristocrat and Wallflower

Regency Romance Adventure

Earl of Wainthorpe — Book 1

Earl of Scarborough — Book 2

Earl of Keyworth — Book 3

Earl of Renshaw — Book 4

HEART OF A SCOT

A Passionate Enemies to Lovers

Scottish Highlander Historical Mystery

Romance Adventure

To Love a Highland Laird — Book 1

To Redeem a Highland Rogue — Book 2

To Seduce a Highland Scoundrel — Book 3

To Woo a Highland Warrior — Book 4

HIGHLAND HEATHER ROMANCING A SCOT: CASTLE BRIDES

A Passionate Enemies to Lovers Second Chance Scottish Highlander Mystery Romance

Wishes and Wonder — Book 9

A Yuletide Highlander — Book 10

SECRETS OF SCANDALOUS LADIES
A Romantic Class Difference Forced Proximity

Regency Romance with Aristocrats

A Lady, A Kish, A Christmas Wish — Book 1

No Lady for the Lord — Book 2

Love Lessons for a Lady — Book 3

His One and Only Lady — Book 4

Never a Proper Lady — Book 5

Lady Tempts a Rogue — Book 6

THE CULPEPPER MISSES
A Humorous Wallflower Family Saga

Regency Romantic Comedy

The Earl and the Spinster — Book 1

The Marquis and the Vixen — Book 2

The Lord and the Wallflower — Book 3

The Buccaneer and the Bluestocking — Book 4

The Lieutenant and the Lady — Book 5

THE HONORABLE ROGUES®
A Second Chance Redeemable Rogue
and Wallflower Regency Romance

A Kiss for a Rogue — Book 1

A Bride for a Rogue — Book 2

A Rogue's Scandalous Wish — Book 3

To Capture a Rogue's Heart — Book 4

The Rogue and the Wallflower — Book 5

A Rose for a Rogue — Book 6

'Twas the Rogue Before Christmas — Book 7

A Rogue Worth the Risk — Book 8

About the Author

Collette Cameron®

USA Today Bestselling author Collette Cameron® is renowned for her captivating, humorous, and heart-warming Scottish and Regency historical romance novels. With over 65 published titles, over 1.4 million books sold around the world, and multiple writing awards to her credit, Collette is a well-known author in the world of historical romance. Readers love her witty and relatable characters including daring rogues, dashing scoundrels, and the strong and spirited heroines who capture their hearts. From the rugged highlands to the refined drawing rooms of Regency England, Collette's novels will transport you to another time and place, where love and adventure are just a page away.

Collette's Sweet-to-Spicy Timeless Romances® are the perfect escape for readers looking for romantic escape, poignant inspiration, engaging humor, and entertaining stories.

Based in the Pacific Northwest, Collette is surrounded by the lush greenery and rainy skies that inspire her writing. She dreams of one day splitting her time between the Pacific Northwest and Scotland. In the meantime, she indulges in her love of all things cobalt blue, dachshunds, chocolate, and of course, crafting her next historical romance.

Blue Rose Romance® LLC
PO Box 167
Scappoose, Oregon 97056 USA
collettecameron.com

If you haven't joined Collette's exclusive mailing list scan the folloing QR Code to sign up!
You'll get access to exclusive content, sneak peeks,
contests, giveaways, and more...
(P.S. No spammy stuff.)

THE *REGENCY ROSE*®

VIP CLUB

Follow Collette on social media.
Scan the following QR Code:

www.ingramcontent.com/pod-product-compliance
Lightning Source LLC
Chambersburg PA
CBHW071933190726
48293CB00004B/1255